Merry
christmas!

Sister Coyote

ALSO BY MARY CLEARMAN BLEW:

Bone Deep in Landscape: Essays on Writing, Reading, and Place

Balsamroot: A Memoir

All But the Waltz: Essays on a Montana Family

Circle of Women (edited with Kim Barnes)

Runaway

Lambing Out

Sister Coyote

MONTANA STORIES

MARY CLEARMAN BLEW

The Lyons Press

A portion of the novella "Sister Coyote" appeared in *North American Re-
view* under the title "Preparation." "Hunter Safety" appeared in an earlier
version in *Four Quarters* under the title "A Lesson in Hunter Safety."

Printed in the United States of America

10 9 8 7 6 5 4 3 2 1

Library of Congress Cataloging-in-Publication Data

Blew, Mary Clearman, 1939–
Sister coyote: Montana stories / Mary Clearman Blew.
p. cm.
ISBN 1-58574-071-3
1. Montana—Fiction.   I. Title.

PS3552.L46 S57 2000
813′.54—dc21
00-028699

For the daughters of summer

Elizabeth
Misty
Rachel
Alathea

And, of course, Brian and Evan

CONTENTS

Sister Coyote

Kids in the Dark

It was nearly nine o'clock at night, and the last of the long white daylight was draining out of the western horizon. Up on the high meadow the air was much colder than it had been at the ranch house down in the cleft of the hills, and Laura, stuck in the cab of the truck between the two boys, was trying to keep from shivering. The familiar was darkening into the grotesque. On every side the ragged shapes of pines hunched under the first stars, overhanging the fence posts and the three strands of barbed wire that enclosed the cropped grass of the meadow. The long days of August were coming to an end, the Montana nights would be closing in, first frost not far off. Laura shivered outright.

Benny was driving the truck in groaning first gear with the headlights off. When the bald tires slipped off the two dirt tracks that angled across the hayfield toward the dark fortress of obscure palisades that by day was the new stack of hay bales, he wrenched the steering wheel over the hump between the tracks, overcorrected, and sent all three kids squashing into each other as the truck listed.

"You guys got the spot ready?" said Benny.

"Lolly's got it," said Jake.

"Well, get it ready. Lolly, how do you think you're going to hold that spot when you're sitting in the middle? Give it to Jake."

"Don't call me Lolly," said Laura. "And I want to hold it. I'm ready."

"She says she's ready. Jesus have mercy."

"Just tell me when to turn it on," said Laura. "That's all you have to do."

"Shut up, will you? Every goddamn deer in Murray County is going to hear you."

"Yeah, and last night you gave me heck for turning it on too quick."

"Jesus have mercy," said Benny. It was his new catch-phrase, he had been saying it all week.

"Just quit yelling at me," said Laura. But she leaned over Jake and held the spotlight out the window of the cab. The uneven wind raised goose bumps along her bare arm. She felt bored. She and the boys had been jacklighting deer every night since the hay had been taken off the high meadow, but they hadn't shot even one, mainly because Benny wouldn't let Jake drive and still insisted on doing most of the shooting himself.

"Go ahead," said Jake. "Shine it along the fence, there."

The spotlight jerked over the fresh stubble of wild grass and alfalfa, fingered the rank growth under the barbed wire, distorted the cheat grass and Canadian thistles into shifting shapes that shone on the surfaces but refused to penetrate the black undersides of juniper that rippled into the pines.

The truck pitched again as Benny, his foot darting from the brake to the foot feed and back again, peered to see where the tracks led.

"Be careful," said Jake. "You're gonna kill the engine."

"I'd sure as hell rather kill my engine than take a chance on high-centering on that rock that's around here somewhere—"

"Hell, that rock's clear on the other side of the hayfield. Don't you know where you're at?"

Benny slammed on the brake and sent everybody pitching into the dash as a black patch of cheat grass seemed to unroll like a ball out of the dwarfed stems and leaves and roll off across the meadow. No, it was not unrolling, but humping along in rapid hump-jumps, its back quivering. Laura followed it with the spot-light.

"Porcupine," she said. "Shall we kill it?"

"See," said Jake. "You did kill the engine. You scared of porcupines?"

"No, we won't kill it! Do you think there'll be a deer left in the whole damn countryside if you go shooting at a goddamn porcupine?"

Laura thought of pointing out to him that you didn't waste bullets on porcupines. She'd never seen anyone try it, but her father said that porcupines could absorb any number of bullets. Their only vulnerable spot was their skulls, and so you killed them with a club, whenever you spotted one, otherwise you'd have livestock with noses full of quills.

Benny ground the key in the ignition while they all held their breath. Sometimes the old truck just didn't want to start after having its clutch dropped. And they were two or three miles from the house, farther than any of them wanted to walk in the dark. But then the truck fired and bucked and crawled along the tracks by the fence.

"Sure going to be glad when this summer's over," said Benny over Laura's head to Jake. "Sure going to be glad to be going back to school. Anything to get away from this fart operation. Oh sure, summer on a ranch, they said. Spend the summer on a ranch, bucking hay bales, building up the old biceps. And they called this a ranch. What a laugh. It's a goddamn porcupine farm."

"You're getting paid," said Jake. "Better than me."

"Wonder how much they think they'd have to pay me another time to spend a summer scratching alfalfa dust out of the crack in my ass and hanging out with a breed and a bitch—"

"Whoa!" said Laura. She was too surprised to say anything else.

"Listen, she's *fourteen*," said Jake. "You want to know what her dad would do if he heard you talking about her like that? You want her to tell?"

"He won't let me come with you guys again," said Laura. "He just about won't let me now. He says you don't have sense enough to keep from getting caught."

"Only if you tell, I might get caught."

"What would you do if the game warden came along right now?"

"Come on, you guys," said solid Jake. "There oughta be some deer on the other side of Ballard's Knob."

Laura had leaned across Jake to brace herself against the open window frame and keep the spotlight more or less steady. She had no intention of telling her father anything that might end the evening deer-poaching adventures with the boys. But now she could smell the essence of horses that always clung to Jake's clothes, feel his hard bronc-riding, bale-bucking thigh, his breath in her hair, his warmth on her legs and ribs, at the same time that she felt the increasing chill of wind and the rigid metal frame against her arm. She was hot and cold at the same time, she thought. How strange.

The wind had begun as a disturbance in the grass and risen into the underbrush, where it agitated the brittle leaves of hawthorns and chokecherries into crackling complaint. Soon it would attack the pines, wring the lament out of the thrashing boughs and make them moan like tortured souls from the timbered ridges. For now it whipped against the truck and sliced through the thin shirt that Laura wore. She shivered, wishing she had brought a jacket, and then, as her nipples contracted from the cold, that she was wearing black satin. She couldn't see Jake's face from her cramped position, half-lying on his lap, but she didn't have to look at Jake, she'd known him all her life. But Benny the ball-handler, Big Ben from the backfield as he advertised himself, paid by the coach to buck bales all summer and build up his muscles, Benny with his blondish hair and his long lower lip was excitement in himself. Laura would be going to the high school in Fort Maginnis in the fall, where the kids listened to Buddy Holly instead of Hank Williams, and what if Ben were to pay attention to her? She knew how her standing would rise because Big Ben had lived, actually *lived*, in the same house with her and worked for her father all summer.

Big Blowhard, as her father had taken to calling him under his breath. He sure wondered when Jake was going to get a bellyful of Big Blowhard, she'd heard her father tell the stack as he hurled a bale in place.

"Look! Eyes!"

Jake started forward, pinning Laura painfully against the dash. But she held tight to the spotlight and kept it aimed at the two gold globes of light that shifted uncertainly against a filigreed black background of hawthorn brush as Benny slammed on the brake and clawed for the rifle.

Hurry. Hurry. Suppose the game warden comes.

She could barely make out the dark slope of neck and head behind the eyes that were transfixed in the beam of the spotlight. She knew the deer couldn't look away from the light, knew that it was mesmerized by light, knew that this deer wouldn't run as long as she held steady, and so she gripped in an ecstasy of concentration, waiting for Benny to take aim.

He was swearing, half-crying. "Oh shit, where's the shells? Jake, I thought you already loaded this goddamn rifle. God damn it—"

His fingers, clumsy with hurry, shoved shells into the magazine. Laura looked away from the eyes, watched Benny. The urgency of the moment was slipping away.

"It's gonna run," said Jake, resigned.

"No it's not—" Benny was throwing open the door, raising the rifle.

But the eyes were gone, broken away from the spell of the spotlight. The whitened circle held moving leaves and empty grass.

"Son of a bitch!"

"You're *never* going to get one," said Laura.

"Shut up," said Jake. "Maybe you won't scare off the next one."

Laura thought at first that Jake was talking to her, and she squirmed around, indignant. Jake, whom she'd always taken for granted—taken for granted was on *her* side. Then she realized that he was talking over her head to Benny.

"This is *my* dad's truck," she said.

"Don't tell me to shut up," said Benny.

Jake shrugged.

"You blanket ass," said Benny. But Jake only waited until Benny started the stalled pickup again and steered where he thought the tracks were, around the Knob. Laura played with the beam of the spotlight, making it bounce off the grass on the meadow's high edge, where the fence held back foot-high pine saplings and an invading growth of chokecherries and buckbrush and poplar suckers. Trash always crowded in, her father said, after the first-growth pine forest had been logged off and its slash burned.

Watch for eyes, she told herself, watch for eyes. But she had half a mind to tell the boys that she was cold and wanted to go home, that they weren't ever going to shoot a deer. The early thrill of lawbreaking, the poaching that her father and Jake's stepfather and all their foothill neighbors had always done but only half-condoned for their children, was fading with the white light of summer. She sighed and aimed the spotlight along the trees, pretending that she was descending into a narrow tunnel of light, with the silhouette pines closing behind her and nothing ahead but the jagged skyline. Trying to rekindle her thrill, she told herself that she and the boys might well be the first travelers ever to venture into this strange night space, yes, this was what it would be like to travel across the moon or one of the stars. Too much imagination, everyone said about Laura.

But what if she and the boys were being observed, what if they were being followed by golden eyes that glowed out of that dark landscape of stars, what if a vast shape out of the future even now lifted its hoof above the shrunken truck and its shrunken occupants.

"I'm cold," she said.

"There's one!" said Jake.

Benny hit the brakes, and they all lurched into each other. He yanked open the door, lifted the now-loaded rifle.

"I'll get this one, by God," he promised through clenched teeth.

Laura held the light steady and watched the shining eyes shift up and down with the nervous tossing of the head. She saw the shadowy shape that contained the eyes, saw how it lifted its feet and set them down, saw how it yearned to run from the invading light.

The rifle cracked.

"I got it!"

Benny bolted out of the pickup and ran with the rifle, and Jake leaped out and ran after him. Laura slid off the seat and ran after the boys through dark, sharp stubble that sliced at her moccasins and her bare ankles. The old excitement was back. He got one!

"Watch out," said Jake, coming to a halt. "It's still alive, don't get too close."

Now she could see the shape in the grass. Its legs tore at the earth as if in flight from the mysterious blinding light. The rifle cracked again, and the deer stopped thrashing, not at once, but with a gradual relaxation, until there was only a gentle fugitive motion in the legs, and then nothing.

Jake had brought the flashlight from the truck. He trained the beam on the dead deer.

It lay in the stubble, its neck thrown forward, its eyes open and already glazed. Laura held her breath as she saw how the fine neck sloped down and then rose into the shoulders and the tender belly that rounded up out of the stalks of grass and alfalfa. And the delicate haunches, soft under the taupe and white of the pelt.

Jake had his knife out. "A yearling doe," he said.

"By God, I got one!" crowed Benny. "Thought I couldn't do it, didn't you."

"I held the light," said Laura absently. She was watching Jake. Jake lifted the doe's head, bringing his knife around in one sweep that parted the hide into two narrow white lips out of which the red blood spewed behind the blade. The head lopped back, the thickening tongue protruded from the mouth, the eyes looked skyward through a filter of dust and bits of leaves.

"That was quite a shot. Do you know that? I must've missed her backbone, because she was still kicking when I got to her. But I dropped her in her tracks, all right. And it was a long ways for a clean shot, do you realize that?"

The doe's legs were stiffening. Jake pulled up first one hind leg and then the other, lopping off the scent glands. Laura saw the small undeveloped teats, and her own nipples tightened— it was the cold air, she thought. Her ankles stung. She had raked them on stunted wild rosebushes on the run from the truck to the kill.

Now Jake was slitting the belly, disemboweling the doe. He cut away the udder and tossed it into the dark grass.

Benny had walked around to watch Jake dress the deer. He nudged a flank with the toe of his cowboy boot. "She's nice and fat, isn't she. She'll make good chops. Hell, that spotlight really stops them in their tracks, doesn't it. They don't know what it is, don't know where to go, don't know anything."

Jake stuck his arm deep into the body cavity. He groped around, pulled his arm away, displayed a small, sticky mass. "Here's the heart."

"Hey, I don't want it!" cried Benny. "Keep that damn thing away from me, I don't want my clothes bled on. Lolly can carry it home if she wants her mom to cook it."

"Hell no, Ben. You earned it," said Jake. He stood remote in the dark, holding out the heart. Going to get more Indian as he gets older, was what her mother always said about Jake. Really it's a pity, she told Laura. Laura tried to see Jake's face, but the flashlight had been stuck on a clump of buckbrush to focus its beam on the carcass of the doe, and both boys had become abstractions with voices but no faces.

"I ain't touching that sucker," said Benny. "No way. No. No, you back off, guy. Don't you try to smear me up with that thing."

Jake had taken a step toward him, holding out the heart on the palm of his hand.

"Back off, man!" cried Benny.

They stood, confronting each other on opposite sides of the illuminated carcass, while time stretched into tension. Benny's tall, wavering shadow, Jake's face lit like a mask as he moved into the flashlight beam. So that's what it's all about, came to Laura like a revelation that fled before she could understand it or even remember it. It's all about them.

What about me? I'm somebody.

She turned to Jake, but Jake was as distant from her as stone. Jake took one more step toward Benny. Benny's whole body seemed to convulse with the effort of his muscles to hold his ground, but it was Benny who backed away and Laura who thought that she would remember Jake's one more step for the rest of her life.

Time snapped back, tension broke. Jake turned and handed the doe's heart to Laura, and she took it, because it was no big deal, it was only the heart of a deer, she had often handled the hearts of deer.

She walked back to the truck, carrying the heart in her hands, holding it well in front of her to keep the blood away from her clothes. At the truck, in the lee of cooling metal, she tipped her head back and turned in a complete circle, but the only light she saw was the cold light of stars. Benny was Benny and Jake was still Jake, whether or not he had stepped over a line between yesterday and all the tomorrows. Holding the doe's heart, she climbed into the cab of the truck.

Hunter Safety

Laura stood in the doorway of the VFW Club and peered into the dark sanctuary of middle-aged men. From along the bar and from tables farther back in the gloom, the drowsy regulars roused themselves to stare at her, the intruder. The overheated old cavern was thick with smoke and the smell of draught beer. Even the football game on the overhead television screen had been turned down so low that the flickering figures in uniforms looked like ghosts from a faraway world of combat come to haunt these sleepy and well-fed veterans.

The bartender hauled himself off his elbows and, squinting against the late afternoon sunshine that flooded through the door behind her, lumbered down the bar toward Laura.

"You bringing a kid to the hunter safety class? They're holding the meeting in the basement. Take the left-hand turn," he advised, and turned back to the game.

Apparently several parents and sons had been searching for the hunter safety course ahead of her and Robin.

Self-conscious and pretending that she did not see the row of sleepy eyes that opened wide enough to track her, Laura sidled past the bar and down the basement stairs. Robin, pretending to be aloof but keeping so close that he was almost trampling her heels, hung on to the paper and pencil he had been instructed to bring along.

She had never been in a VFW Club. The odor of men going about their male doings made her feel as edgy as a hunted thing herself, even though she had seen them replete and satiated with beer. The lighted basement, with its Sheetrocked walls and echoing cement floor, recalled less taboo church suppers-and-bingo, but Laura still felt like an alien. Her old dread of opening a door upon a roomful of strangers kept her lingering at the foot of the stairs, examining a thirty-year-old tinted aerial photograph of VFW headquarters in Pennsylvania that must have been hung before Vietnam, when this club was wide awake and alive.

"Mother!" muttered Robin in her ear, and Laura opened the door.

Nothing had prepared her for the din. It was still only five minutes to seven, but the room was packed with perhaps fifty squirming boys and a few girls. The racket made her think wildly of a giant chicken house. She could not take her hand off the doorknob. Never had she encountered so much undirected energy, not among her clients in the drunk tank, certainly not in morning court. Boys boiled through the room and erupted in spurts of arguments or scuffles over the one or two remaining chairs. All the folding seats set out along the tables for the meeting had been seized by early arrivals who glared defiantly at prowling latecomers.

"I see now why they never advertise this class," said Laura over her shoulder to Robin.

Robin ignored her. Completing the hunter safety course was the only way he could get a license to hunt before he was sixteen, and he had made up his mind that he was going to get a license.

"Over there," he said. Laura, following the jerk of his head, saw a row of metal filing cabinets which offered a place to perch at the back of the room. Robin swung himself up and sat, legs dangling, on top of one of the cabinets. After an involuntary glance over her shoulder to see if she was making herself conspicuous, Laura scrambled up beside him. Her legs dangled beside Robin's, exactly the same length as his, as like his as a twin in washed-out blue Levi's and cowboy boots.

But once she was high and dry in the corner, Laura felt enough at ease to watch the crowd. In the next ten minutes another twenty or thirty boys and a few fathers came down the basement stairs, looked bewildered, and let themselves be sucked into the maelstrom. Packed against each other, two or three deep along the walls or hunkering down in corners, boys jostled each other for space.

The policeman who taught the hunter safety class, Fred Flisch, was wearing an ordinary sports shirt and tan pants this evening, but he gripped a short rod like a swagger stick in front of him, and everybody knew who he was. His eyes, a pair of pebbles sunken into a porterhouse face, roamed over the racketing ten- and twelve- and fourteen-year-olds, counting them, and the boys sneered back at him, bright-eyed.

The three or four other adults in the room, fathers, were leaning back against the walls, resigned to the few minutes they had to spend in bedlam before they could get away and have a few beers until time to pick up their kids again. Meanwhile they shrugged and exchanged glances, glad it was Flisch and not themselves who had to face this bunch of brats. Mean little devils! Oh, everybody's kid was all right by himself, of course. Really decent kids. But a pack like this, all these kids at once? And Fred Flisch might be an ornery son of a bitch himself, but hell! Who else would tackle a job like this?

Flisch continued to pace the room, his back as broad and thick as a prime steer's, his pebble eyes counting the children.

Laura glanced at her son, wondering what he was thinking. Robin's face was unreadable under his heavy thatch of black hair. That was Robin, watching the world through skeptical dark eyes that never missed a thing and never gave a thing away. When he was a toddler, strangers had stopped to look at the striking little boy with the beautiful dark eyes. Now at thirteen he was beautifully proportioned, with the beginnings of a mustache on his upper lip. He was growing almost visibly. In a few months Laura wouldn't be able to lend him a pair of clean Levi's the way she had this evening. But the surge of good feeling came back to remind her: at least she had done a good job with Robin.

She felt someone watching her from across the room and looked up to see Flisch's assistant, a beefy young man with a blond crew cut and jowls like Flisch's. He wore a fluorescent orange hunting vest, as buoyant as a life jacket. Laura had noticed him earlier. He had pretended to be counting stacks of hunter-safety booklets, but all the while he had stolen looks at the pandemonium, and she had recognized his unease as teachers' stage fright.

Now she dropped her eyes. She supposed he knew something about her. Or at least he knew her by the labels that this town still applied to the women of the seventies. Divorced. Lawyer. Liberal.

Or maybe it was just that not many women came to the hunter safety class. Probably it was usually fathers and sons.

Boys kept pushing into the room, trampling heedlessly and raising tides of protest from kids crowded leg to leg and back to back on the floor. Laura thought there surely must be a hundred kids in the room by now. The air was getting almost too depleted to breathe.

At five to seven Flisch stopped his pacing. His knuckles glistened on his short rod. "How many of you kids are under twelve?" he demanded.

About half the pack raised a hand, and then they all looked around to see if their friends were raising their hands, took their own hands down, argued with their neighbors over how old they were, changed their minds.

"All you guys under twelve, you're gonna have to leave. We're gonna run another class in a few weeks. You can take hunter safety then."

"Awww!" rose the wail. Everybody wanted to take the class right now. Right now!

"If you're under twelve, you can't go hunting this year, anyway. You have to be at least twelve before you're legal. You can come back in a few weeks. We'll have another class organized."

At last about thirty of the younger boys were chased out, complaining as they went. Even then, there weren't enough application forms to go around, and Flisch's assistant went to bring another stack.

Robin was passed an application card and an instruction manual. Laura got an orange NRA booklet entitled *When Your Boy or Girl Asks for a Gun.* The sketch of the smiling father and son on the cover reminded her of a picture from a child's primer.

Robin scowled at the booklet from under his shag of dark hair. "They ought to have a picture of the dad in his undershirt, yelling how he'll break the kid's head if he doesn't shut up," he hissed in her ear.

"Robin!" said Laura. "You'd better be quiet."

But to herself she was pleased. Robin had never bogged down in the slough of the predictable where so many of her young clients seemed permanently mired. At least she had taught him to question, to consider, to think for himself. Robin would never settle for labels.

Flisch's assistant, sounding angry as he raised his voice to be heard, explained how the application card must be filled out, where the parent or guardian must sign, and how the kids could get their hunting licenses at half-price if they asked for student tags and showed their hunter safety cards. Robin had filled out his card before the assistant could finish his explanation. He handed it to Laura to sign.

"Where'd you say to put our names?" shouted a very small boy from the back of the room.

His cry loosed a torrent.

"We supposed to turn these in now?"

"What'd you say?"

"What'd you say?"

"Hold it down!" Flisch bellowed. He patrolled the room, stepping over legs and gripping his little rod, while his assistant explained everything all over again. Laura turned the application card over and looked at the answers that Robin had filled in with his cramped penmanship.

"Do you really want to do this?" she couldn't help asking. Because at first she had thought he was joking when he announced that he was going to attend the hunter safety class and get his hunting license. Even now she wasn't certain that he was serious. Looking at him, she was struck, as she had been a thousand times, at how much Robin looked like her. Of course his coloring came from his father. But the velvety fringed eyes and the soft skin, even the rounded arms and legs under the denim shirt and the blue Levi's washed to velvet were the same size as hers. Robin was a part of her, exactly like her except for the silken mustache beginning to claim his upper lip like insidious, growing maleness.

"Mother!" said Robin, annoyed. "*You* hunted."

"That's why I don't want you doing it."

"We already talked about it. And Granddad's counting on it." He reached over and repossessed the card she already had signed.

Now Flisch was explaining the requirements for passing the hunter safety course while his assistant took a turn at prowling up and down, getting bumped and kicked by legs and elbows while he tried to outstare the faces with the impudent grins. His flustered gaze strayed to Laura on her file-cabinet perch, and again she willed herself still.

All the children had to pass the hunter safety course before they could get a hunting license. That much Flisch could hold over them. Otherwise no legal hunting, no going out with a rifle until they were sixteen.

He read aloud a list of rules called the Ten Commandments of Hunting.

"You will know these by heart," he said, glaring around at the smirking boys who had crawled around behind him to lie on their stomachs. "Word for word. We're gonna give you a test afterward, and you have to get an 88 on it to pass. The national requirement, it's only 80, but here in Blaine County we say you have to get an 88."

One boy raised his hand. "What if we don't?"

His friends tittered, as delighted as if he had posed an unanswerable dilemma.

"Then you don't get no hunting license. And furthermore. It don't matter what you do get on that test. Even if you get 100 percent on that written test, it still don't matter. We got to sign it where it says you passed. And if we catch one of you pulling *some stunt*"—he paused to let the words sink in, walking three paces with his rod gripped hard in front of his belly, while the boys behind him caught each others' eyes and quivered with their held-in giggles—"we catch you pulling *some stunt*, you're never gonna get no license. We'll pull your card and that'll be the end of it, no matter what you get on that written test. And there won't be no way you can hunt until you're sixteen."

The boys began to snicker openly. Fights broke out all over the room, intensified by the heat and the press of young bodies intruding against others. They punched each other, pretending that they were being funny about it, but the glitter in their eyes gave them away. Application cards were being snatched, torn, spun from hand to hand. Noise rose like a tidal wave, and Laura, crouching back on her file cabinet, remembered the men in the bar upstairs, entrenched over their beer and lulled by the silent combat of the televised football game. It was a wonder that the ceiling didn't buckle under them.

"All right, all right! Let's keep it down!" shouted Flisch. He and his assistant stalked up and down the room, their faces pulled into masks that threatened a grim fate to whelps who failed to take hunter safety seriously. The weight of their expressions dragged the children nearest them to order, but laughing and slapping and punching broke out as soon as they moved on. And yet there had been a change. The children's antagonism toward each other had turned into united defiance of the adults.

"That prick Flisch is gonna get his!" hissed Robin. Laura, glancing at him, saw that her son's eyes gleamed out of a face as flushed as the other children's.

"Robin!" she said, appalled.

"Well, you know what he did to Mike Worrick's brother! I suppose you think that's great. I suppose you think a kid *deserves* to have his ribs broken by a cop."

"I didn't say that!" began Laura in an angry whisper, but Robin already had withdrawn from the argument. He was listening sardonically to Flisch, who had launched himself on a patriotic tangent.

"We live in a great state. The greatest. You want to appreciate Montana? Then you go someplace else to live for a while and try to go hunting or fishing. You're gonna run into garbage everywhere you go, and you're gonna meet people who got no respect for anybody or anything. You gotta go see it to believe it."

Robin's eyes slid around to see how Laura was reacting.

"What's the matter?" she whispered, knowing he was testing her.

"Nothing."

He withdrew again, offended. Laura could feel from the stiff flesh of his young neck and arms that he was pained at her refusal to share his disgust. And yet she sensed still another barrier. Would Robin *let* her agree with him? From across the room Flisch's assistant, almost submerged by the turbulence of the pack in spite of his billowing orange jacket, also was watching her, and Laura kept her face a careful blank.

The current story going around the law office about Fred Flisch had to do with a college house party he had raided a few weeks ago. The kids had had no warning and couldn't get rid of whatever it was, mescaline or something—or worse yet, according to the preferred version among Laura's clients, they would have had plenty of time to flush whatever it was down the toilet except that Flisch had bulled his way inside the house, illegally, and worked over a couple of the boys. It was said that one of the boys had had a cracked rib, another a ruptured spleen. Laura hadn't believed the story when she first heard it. Not that Flisch was incapable of it. She could believe almost anything of those slow furious eyes and those meaty hands locked on their rod. But surely no parent would remain silent at such injury?

Laura caught herself hoping that they all had responsible fathers and then realized that she, Flisch, and Flisch's assistant were the only adults in the room. All the fathers had dropped off their children and made their escapes. She must have been dreaming about the father-son sketch on the cover of the hunter safety booklet. The basement seethed tonight with the hostility of sixty or more boys who were, it was beginning to sink in for Laura, after a few more meetings like this one, to be armed with rifles and loosed upon the countryside for hunting season with cards stating that the possessor knew the Ten Commandments of Hunting, had passed the written test with a score of at least an 88, and hadn't been caught at any stunts.

"After all," Flisch was telling the boys, "we've been around for a while. We've seen a thing or two. We're just telling you, same as your dads would. And we aren't always perfect, I wouldn't try to tell you that. We don't always bring in the game. We get skunked once in a while, same as your dads do sometimes. No," he conceded. "We're not perfect."

"Don't you listen to him," spoke up his assistant. His mouth smiled while his eyes roved anxiously back and forth above the ruckus, looking for rapport with the pack, any at all. "Him"— he turned sad brown eyes on Flisch—"him, he got a nice six-point elk last year. Me, I was the one that got skunked."

His laugh, divided between Flisch and the pack, begged them all to be guys together, one good bunch of people.

"Wonder if I should tell him what my dad got!" sneered Robin.

"Robin!" said Laura. For once she was more disturbed than secretly pleased at his jab at his father. The tide below her was swelling, and it seemed to her that not even Flisch could keep a semblance of order much longer.

Flisch had begun a lecture on how hunters should clean up after themselves. "It makes me sick to find garbage every-where. Even way out in the hills! Probably dumped by one of those that don't have no respect for this country or themselves either. But if I catch any of you throwing pop cans or *whathaveyou*"—again the long rhetorical pause, the glare around the room—"or *whathaveyou*, I'll skin you myself."

Flisch's assistant began to tell a story.

"Some of you may know Steve Lambert? He owns Quality Western Wear, here in town? Well, his father, old Saylor Lambert, he's got a ranch down by Fort Maginnis, down in Murray County."

Laura's attention was distracted from Robin. Murray County was where she had grown up, and she remembered Saylor Lambert as an old man who kept a tight thumb on what he owned.

"Old Saylor, he's got him a fishing pond on that ranch of his. We went down there, me and Mr. Flisch"—the sad eyes made the acknowledgment—"and we fished his pond. We didn't have no luck. And beings that I wasn't getting no bites, I figured I may as well do something. So I gets me one of them onion sacks, made of net, like I always carry with me in the camper, and I starts to gathering up beer cans and all kinds of crap from around that pond."

"Pretty soon here comes old man Lambert in his pickup. 'I been watching you boys through my field glasses from the top of that hill,' he says. 'You seen the guys that threw all this garbage around my pond?' "

" 'No,' I says. 'I ain't seen nobody. But I've been gathering up their garbage for the last hour.' "

" 'I know you have,' he says to me. 'I've been watching you. And I want you to know, any time you want to hunt or fish on my land, that's fine. You boys are always welcome. But that son of a bitch that left that garbage here, I'm gonna shoot the son of a bitch if I catch him. That's what I've been doing on top of that hill. Laying for him.' "

Boys were shouting all around the room. Laura could not hear the end of the story, or the moral, if it had a moral.

"Sick!" sneered Robin, and she turned on him, but just then another fight broke out in the corner behind the file cabinets. A boy, catapulted by a companion's shove, crashed into Laura and recovered himself without ever being aware of her. He threw himself at the boy who had shoved him just as Robin launched himself silently at his back.

"Robin!" cried Laura.

"Hold it down!" bellowed Flisch. "You can quiet down for another few minutes. We're just about out of time tonight."

Somehow his voice just overrode the tide. He soldiered on, giving instructions about the next class meeting and what the boys should bring with them. He promised pictures of hunting accidents: "We'll let you see just what it looks like to have half of your head blown off because you used the wrong gauge shell in your shotgun."

By now every boy in the room was baying at his neighbor, but the effect was for Flisch. Their eyes were fixed on Flisch, their mouths frozen in grins while they waited for him to make his move. Robin leaned against the file cabinets with his young shoulders quivering. Even on her high perch, Laura was jostled again, and then Robin was shoved back against her, pinning her legs at a painful angle between his shoulder blades and the front of the cabinets. He lunged back, daring the other boy.

Flisch's assistant had retreated to the row of locked gun cabinets at the rear of the basement. His widened eyes found Laura's again, and Laura abruptly drew her knees up against her chest and hugged herself on her small threatened island. The other adults had been wise to depart, she realized. Afraid of their own children and willing to let someone else try to brutalize them into obedience.

"Same time tomorrow night!" shouted Flisch. "Don't forget to learn your Ten Commandments!"

Then, finally, he yielded to volume. He stepped aside, let the pack storm the stairs.

Laura waited on her high-and-dry file cabinet until the basement was cleared of all but the stragglers who had already lost their application cards or had them snatched away. Robin surfaced from a hooting tangle of arms and legs and fought his way to Flisch to turn in his card.

Laura slid off the cabinet and waited for Robin. Maybe she shouldn't have signed his card, after all. But she knew she couldn't have denied him. She would have been acting like a nervous mother, hovering over the boy growing up without a father in the house. Everyone knew it was her fault he didn't have a father in the house. The least she could do was see to it that he grew up normally.

Flisch took Robin's card. In the sudden calm, his eyes, weary in his overfed face, flicked over Laura and registered nothing. He seemed deflated. The electric light fell straight down from the ceiling; he didn't even cast a shadow.

After all, nothing had happened.

"Mother!" said Robin. His face glowed. "Can I go with Mike?"

"Mike who?"

"Mike Worrick."

"I thought you and I were going out for pizza afterward."

"Yes, but—Mother! Those guys are going to the Dairy Queen. And I can walk home with Mike."

They were halfway up the basement stairs, Robin a step ahead of her. Laura had to look up to meet his hot, urgent eyes.

"I don't know," she said. She remembered how she had worried whether he would ever make friends his own age.

Someone was climbing the stairs behind them.

Laura hastily made way for Flisch's assistant. "Excuse me," she said.

"That's okay," said the young man. His arms were full of slippery hunter safety pamphlets. Trying to keep from dropping them, he followed Laura and Robin out of the basement.

"Mother!" Robin urged.

"All right. Go ahead. Watch out for the traffic on Fifth. It's getting dark."

"Can I have money for a hamburger?"

Laura dug in her pocket and found a five-dollar bill. The younger Worrick boy, she noticed, was waiting in the doorway of the VFW Club. A few other boys lingered on the street corner, waiting for a ride or perhaps killing time on their own.

"Some class, right?"

It was the young man, Flisch's assistant.

"I wouldn't want to try to teach it," Laura agreed. Robin had snatched the five-dollar bill and run off with Mike.

"Yeah," he leaned against the wall with his armload of pamphlets, making conversation. "A lot of folks think Fred, he's too damn rough on those kids. But you saw what it was like."

"Yes."

"And it's worse, other places. You know there's city schools where they got policemen right there in the halls?"

"Yes," said Laura. "I knew that."

"Hell, some adult's got to be in charge. Only thing is, when the adult's you, and you know you got no answers, it makes you wonder. Right?"

He risked a laugh.

"Yes," said Laura for the third time. She remembered the panic of her first year of practice.

The young man waited, trying to think of something else to say. Laura thought of him, armed with a nylon net sack that once had contained onions, attacking the edge of an avalanche of garbage.

"You wouldn't care to stay and have a beer?" he asked.

"No," she said politely. "I've got to go home and read briefs."

It was almost dark. The streetlights cast circles of light down the avenue, but the September wind was sharp against the corners of buildings and parked cars. Children still roamed the streets. A parting jeer floated back through the evening gloom. Somewhere ahead was Robin. Laura braced herself as she left the dusty shelter of the VFW Club and made her way into the chill.

Bears and Lions

Places of great scenic beauty always seem to be hard to make a living on, and certainly that has been true of our ranch. My father tried cattle, sheep, a little logging, but even in my childhood our life here was marginal. My father is dead now, and my mother lives in a subsidized apartment in the town of Fort Maginnis, and my sisters have gone away to cities, but my husband and I keep on ranching. We still raise a few sheep, and of course we have the horses. Most years we try to put up a little hay and harvest some oats, but the growing season is so short, here in the foothills of Montana's Snowies, that crops often don't ripen before first frost. I don't even try to raise a garden. But James and I cut our own logs to build this house on a south slope, above the county road, and from our living room windows we can look down at the old overgrown hay meadows where, at twilight, deer slip in and out of the hawthorn brush and the poplar saplings and vanish into the pines on the steep hill.

"It's so beautiful here," my oldest sister says when she visits, and then she shakes her head. "But how long can you and James hold out?"

And the ranch really is beautiful, only seven miles from Fort Maginnis on a gravel road that winds along Castle Creek through groves of aspens and ravines of haws and chokecherries and wild roses, always within sight and sound of the great pines that heave and murmur in the air currents of summer and will turn mute and ink-dark with the winter snows. But the truth is that we couldn't afford the ranch if it weren't for our jobs. We own eight hundred and fifty acres, which sounds wonderful to the teachers I assist at Sacajawea School down in Fort Maginnis, but too many of those acres are sidehills that were logged off long ago and now hold little but scrub pine growing through the ancient slash. I sometimes worry whether the income from the ranch will stretch to pay the taxes. James and I heat our house with wood we cut ourselves, and I shop at the Goodwill. James delivers mail three days a week on a hundred-mile rural route, and I am a teachers' aide. Our salaries buy groceries and pay the phone and electric bills and stretch to provide Park and Steve with some of their hearts' desires, like baseball gear and Walkmans and Nintendos and their own rifles. Like all kids' lists, theirs are endless.

"Oh but Val, what a great place to raise the boys," say the teachers in the lounge during their free hour, and I know it's true.

For instance, that day last summer when James and I and the boys rode as far as Castle Butte, looking for horses. The draft mares had broken through a fence and gotten lost, and Park and I had split off from James and Steve to search that high flat stretch we call Ballard's Knob, which was a meadow once, on the old Ballard place, but now is grown over with aspens and pine seedlings, stirrup-high and higher. To restore it to pasture would take a bulldozer and defoliant, and it wouldn't be worth it, it wouldn't be economical, not for a short season of wild grass. A consortium of doctors own the Ballard land now, and they've torn out the old fences so they can drive up from Billings every fall and go hunting, but they don't rub shoulders with us locals. The Ballards have been gone for years, and so have most of the old neighbors from my father's time, and our new neighbors down on Castle Creek commute to jobs in Fort Maginnis and build cabins from kits on ten-acre plots and hope to keep their kids away from drugs by living in the country.

My father had known that a time was coming when ordinary people couldn't make a living in the foothills. "Don't want to live to see it," he always said, and he didn't.

I had been thinking about Father as I rode, and how he would have growled at Park for goofing off, riding cross-legged in the saddle and letting old Sandy snatch a bite of bunchgrass any time she felt like it. And I thought how the high pastures would have seemed just the same to Father in so many ways—the stir of the wind through the scrub, the sandstone boulders rising to meet the ramparts of Castle Butte, the distant blue outline of the Snowies, the blue, blue sky and rolling clouds. And yet all was so altered, so stark, without traces of human habitation, that I was beginning to feel as though I had ridden into forbidden territory and might, just might, catch a glimpse of some parallel world through gauze or mist or smoke. And then, as though roused by Father's voice inside my head, something rippled through the undergrowth, some fleeing animal.

What? I reined in my mare, stood in my stirrups to see what disturbed the buckbrush. That dark shape, that furry shape that humped like a raccoon as it ran, but bigger and faster than any raccoon, and then I knew. A bear cub, where no bear had been seen for years and years and years, perhaps ever.

I tried to speak, to call to Park to look, and perhaps I did. I spurred my mare into a canter and followed the cub to the edge of the Knob, where the pasture falls off in a slope, and there, in a sunny patch of grass and mountain geraniums, where she had been digging, surprised and rising on her hind legs to get a better look at me, was the sow.

She seemed unafraid. She stood, no further from me on my horse than the width of a residential street, while the slight breeze disturbed the grass and the pink blooms of the wild geraniums and ruffled her fur. The part of my mind that had separated from me and raced ahead to its own surmise now called back from a distance to ask why, in a good year, did she have only the one cub that had stopped, trembling, to get his own look at me. I had time to think how beautiful she was, with her black fur shading to a sunburned rust, with her serene golden eyes watching me from her own dimension. And then I saw the dark furball clinging to the top of a pine tree at the foot of the slope, the other cub.

"Wow, Mom, bears!" breathed Park, who had kicked old Sandy into a trot and caught up with us. "Cool, Mom!"

I may have blinked, I may have turned to catch the expression on Park's face. In the next moment the breeze stirred empty grass and aspen leaves. The bears had vanished. And I felt awe, and an ache for the deserted grass and the absence of what I had just witnessed. Never, never, had I dreamed that I would come face to face, as though with a wild neighbor, with a bear sow and her cubs in the Castle Butte pasture.

"Were your horses afraid?" asked my oldest sister over the telephone from Seattle when I called to tell her about the bears.

"No. It was the strangest thing. You always read that horses are so terrified of bears, but they just stood there and watched."

"They've probably known all along that the bears are there. They've gotten used to their scent."

"That's what James thinks."

"Ironic, isn't it? The old settlers thought they were clearing out trees and wildlife to make a safe and settled place, and now they're gone and the bears are back. But where are they *coming* from? I mean, I never imagined seeing bears in the foothills when we were all growing up, and I never heard of anybody else who did. What's going on? Is it part of some species reintroduction program?"

"James thinks that there have always been a few bears in the Snowies, not many, but a few. In the years that there was a bounty on them, they were hunted hard, but now the bounties are gone, and just the other way around, if you want to hunt a bear, you buy a fifty-dollar tag and draw for a permit. So the bears in the mountains have increased, and their range is over-crowded, and more and more are moving down into the foothills with us."

"So it's political."

"Maybe, but sometimes it seems more personal. I was thrilled to see her and the cubs, but I won't feel so thrilled if she bothers our sheep."

A long silence on the line, and I wondered what Laura was thinking. She often sees so many sides of what seems obvious to James and me, like what will happen when wolves are reintroduced into cattle and sheep country.

But finally she said, "Do you remember the Canadian lynx that Father shot?"

Years ago. The last summer Laura spent on the ranch, so she would have been seventeen and I would have been nine, the same age Park is now. I remember that it was very early in the morning, our reflections in the kitchen window fading to gray light, and Laura was serving breakfast to Father, who was drinking coffee to prime himself for his day's work. He growled something at me, to behave myself, and Laura brought the pot and poured him a second cup of coffee. On her way back to the stove, she stopped at the window, rigid.

"What's that?" she whispered.

Father glanced casually along the line of her gaze, then tensed as though he'd woken fully alive for the first time in years. He shoved his chair back from the table and crossed the kitchen in three strides, lifted down the rifle, the 30.06, from its rack above the refrigerator, and pumped a shell into its chamber as he tiptoed across the creaking floorboards of the old screened porch and eased the door open.

I was right behind him, wanting to see what was happening. The gray predawn light had concentrated in a pink stain behind the log shed, and what at first I thought was a shadow had detached itself from the squat shape of the tractor beside the shed. Then the shadow moved again, taking on a form with a current as powerful as an electric surge, which any country-raised child, even a nine-year-old, recognizes as life, wild life.

Father had braced his left hand on the doorjamb, was taking aim. My heart was pounding on the same frequency as the electric surge. *Get it, Father!*

Then the explosion of the rifle, reverberating inside my head, expanding the porch, echoing from the opposite pine slopes. At first I felt more blinded than deafened, and then my eyes cleared, and the sound of the explosion died away, and the world was still the world.

My mother was running downstairs in her wrapper. "What are you shooting at?"

We all went across the road to look.

Father was a dead shot in those days, and he had hit the lynx in the heart, killing her instantly. The smallest dark stain of blood had oozed from the bullet hole just back of her foreleg, and in the growing daylight we all marveled at the dappled taupe and cream of her fur and the fading gold glare of her eyes. I was hopping around, beside myself with excitement. Father lifted the lynx by her scruff, holding her at shoulder height so her hind pads just brushed the dirt, while my mother ran to get the camera to take pictures as soon as there was enough light, and I felt the tips of the lynx's claws and studied the dirt stuck to her dulled eyes and petted the wild tufts of her ears.

* * *

"Why do you think he shot it, Val?" my sister asked, over the long distance line from Seattle.

"Because he was worried that it would bother the sheep."

"But he always said he'd never seen a Canadian lynx down here in Montana, that he supposed this one was passing through the country on its way north. Why did he have to shoot it, if it was just passing through?"

Later I thought about the unspoken questions and answers that limned the ones we spoke aloud. Probably there was a bounty on lynxes at that time, fifty or even a hundred dollars, and probably Father sold the pelt for another fifty or a hundred dollars down at Pacific Hide and Fur.

It was always money with Father, she says.

You don't understand, I want to tell my sister. You went off to live in Seattle, where weather is never worse than a nuisance, and wild animals never take bites out of your salary. You can afford to take the long view. James and I have a living to make, and we have a right to protect our livestock.

But this is about more than money, Val.

That's true. Father shot that lynx because she was calling for his bullet. Calling as strong as a power surge. I felt it that morning, and so did you, my sister.

* * *

Today when I come across the article in the newspaper, I call my sister and read it to her over the telephone, about the five-year-old boy in western Montana who was fatally mauled by a mountain lion a hundred yards from his front door. And his body dragged off into the underbrush, where it was found a day later by a sheriff's search party, partially devoured . . .

"God!" says my sister. "But yes, that story was on the news here, too."

Then she tells me about a partner in her law practice who claims that the child's death was the fault of people building subdivisions on old game trails, interfering with centuries-old migratory patterns of wildlife and bringing fatal conflicts upon themselves.

My anger surges up so suddenly that it is a moment before I can trust my voice. "Does he think that if those parents had just moved their house back a few yards, the mountain lion would have stayed on his centuries-old migratory path and not attacked their child?"

"Pretty stupid, I guess."

"Does he know anything about the size of a mountain lion's hunting range?"

My sister sighs. She is trying not to quarrel. "Do you have mountain lions on the ranch now?"

"We haven't seen them. But lions are stalkers, you know. James is sure that he's been watched while he's been working in the timber. He's seen lion tracks, and he's found deer carcasses where some animal has come back more than once to feed, which means it wasn't coyotes. We've been concerned enough to teach Park and Steve what to do if they happen to meet a lion."

"Which is to do what?"

"To stand still. Slide their jackets down over their arms, then raise them over their heads to make themselves look as big as possible. To make a lot of noise. And whatever they do, not to run. Any sudden movement will activate the lion's instinct to pounce, just like any cat."

"When I was growing up on the ranch," says my sister, softly, "I used to slip off in the afternoons with my horse and a book, and I'd dream that I was following a trail through the timber, with a rifle, to protect myself from bears and mountain lions. And it gave me a thrill. But I always knew I was just pretending, that I'd never really see a bear or a lion."

"For Park and Steve, it isn't dream danger."

"I understand that much," she says.

In the nature encyclopedia we bought for the boys, it says that attacks by mountain lions on humans are rare and usually attributed to animals that are sick or weak and can't catch other game, or animals that are suffering from rabies. It also says that most of the deer killed by mountain lions are diseased or crippled.

Park, who has a science report to write, reads carefully and then looks up. "The lions are nature's way of culling the deer herds, right, Dad?"

James studies the chunk of heart pine he's about to toss into the wood stove as though he expects to read an answer in the splinters. Here we are, it's only September, and already the rain is freezing, and we're stoking the stove at night and firing it up again to take the chill off the house in the mornings. James collects his thoughts, tosses the wood to the flames, and answers Park.

"Now with wolves, they chase down their game, so naturally it's the slow deer they catch first, and so wolves do cull the herds, some. But with a critter like a lion that stalks his game, and when he's strong and quick enough to bring down a full-grown buck deer with antlers, like the one I found back of the ridge, it's more bad luck than lack of speed for whichever deer happens to pass under his perch."

"Sheep, hogs, and colts have been killed by mountain lions, although usually in areas where deer have been eliminated," Park reads aloud.

"Well . . . ," says James, noncommittal. He pours hot water over his powdered coffee, sets the kettle back on the wood stove, stirs, settles himself in his rocking chair, picks up his own book, and finds his place.

"Dad," insists Park, "a mountain lion couldn't kill a horse. Could it?"

James lays down his book. "Well . . . yes, it could."

"Could it kill *Sandy?*"

"Come on, Park," I tell him. "Let Dad read."

James runs his fingers through his hair, which is beginning to curl around his collar. He lets his hair and beard grow every winter, gets a haircut and shaves again when the weather turns warm in the spring. I worry about the gray in James's hair and the lines in his face.

"A mountain lion *could* kill Sandy, but it won't as long as Sandy's got sense enough to stay out of the trees and graze in open pasture," James explains. "What a mountain lion does is hide and pounce. Just like a cat does. See?"

And he points out to the kitchen, where Steve is teasing the surviving kitten, which crouches and watches from the seat of a chair while Steve drags a knitting needle along the linoleum. Suddenly the kitten reaches down with a lightning paw and bats the knitting needle out of Steve's hand, nearly falling off the chair in the process. Recovering, it regards us with its dreamy gaze.

Me? Lose my balance? It never happened.

I laugh, but I also remember the scene in the barn this morning when Park found the other kitten dead. I had been down in the lower corral, breaking the rime of ice out of the horses' water trough, and I came blowing on my hands and stamping my feet through the broken-hinged door to find the two boys, desolate.

Park had lifted the dead kitten out of the manger. He held it out to me, wordless. It was frozen stiff. Later, when James examined it, he said a weasel had probably killed it, because its blood had been sucked. At the time, I looked at the draggled gray fur on the rigid little corpse, and then at the faces of my two boys, and my breath hung white in the chill air.

Steve was cradling the other kitten in his arms. "Please, Mom! Can't she come inside and live in the house? We don't want her to die, too!"

I was already shaking my head.

"Please, Mom! Please, please, please?"

"We could get a cat box like people in town have for their cats, and put litter in it, and I'd clean it, honestly I would, Mom, please?"

"Please?"

Steve is the one of our boys who looks like the old photograph that was taken of Father when he was five, with eyes so pure and light, and hair so blond that it looks silver in the photograph. Park looks like James, with darker blond hair and transparent skin that holds its tan even deep into winter. They stood in the freezing barn with anxious faces, pleading, and I thought about what Father would have said about cats in the house, and how grouchy he had gotten during his last years, and about good, tired James, and how patient with Father he had been.

"Okay, but you have to promise to feed it and clean up after it and keep it off the bed," I said, and saw their faces break into smiles through the tears.

"We promise, we promise!"

"Oh yay, yay, yay!"

And Steve thrust the surviving kitten at me. It sank its needle claws into the front of my insulated coveralls and clung to me, blank-eyed.

Now, as I watch the kitten play with Steve, lunging at the knitting needle and batting it out of his hands, I realize that I'll soon be lucky to have a straight needle left to knit with. And I look at my little family, James absorbed in his book, Park finishing his homework and turning on the TV, the wood stove radiating warmth in the enclosure of bare floorboards and exposed insulation where we haven't been able to afford Sheetrocking yet, and the black windows mirroring us back through the leaves of coleus and philodendron and spider plants and ficus, and I think that I would like to tell my sister, so what if my only kitchen counter is a home-hewed plank?

Then the thud on the roof.

James looks up with his face so intent that I can't tell myself that I heard nothing. He sits listening with his finger marking the place in his book and the electric light deepening the lines in his face. Park is absorbed in *Rescue 911* and oblivious.

"Turn that down, will you, Park?" says James. Park stares. James lays down his book and gets up out of his chair. He pauses by the gun rack that holds Father's old rifle, the 30.06, and Father's shotguns and James's own .250 Savage, but he leaves the guns on the rack and goes to stand by the window with his face close to the glass.

I can hear nothing, only the snap of a pine knot in the fire. Steve has stopped playing with the cat. The familiar room has taken on a fresh intensity, and I find myself counting the scars and gouges on the chair legs, thinking that I really should sand them down and varnish them. Outdoors the wind has picked up, and the muted roar from the ridges, where the big pines toss and heave in the dark, sounds as familiar to me and yet as alien as the rumble of traffic might be to someone who lives under a freeway. Behind the house the diamond willow shakes its bare twigs, whines and rattles against the logs as it always does in the wind. But I hear no further thud on the roof, no creak of shingles, no stealthy pad of paws over my head.

"Can't see a thing from here," says James in a neutral voice, turning from the window, "what with the overhang of the eaves."

From some strange vantage point I visualize the night. The frozen mud of our driveway, the parked and dark Blazer, and the looming shapes of our clutter: tractor tires and burning barrel, feed buckets and James's overshoes and the motor from the generator and the shovel. The diamond willow, lashing at the solid house, and, like a barn cat magnified by a power of ten, crouched above the eaves and watching the lighted windows and the flickers of movement, the great shadowy beast from the wild world outside ours.

"Don't go outside!"

"I wasn't planning on it," James says. He stops at the sight of the boys' dumb faces. "Well, now, I wonder. Were either of you fellows thinking about playing a hand of cards before bedtime?"

And I understand the part that falls to me. Acting as if this is a normal evening. Finishing the dishes. Setting the boys' thermoses in the refrigerator, making sure that Park has put his homework in his backpack, seeing to all the small tasks that will ease the Monday morning rush. Getting ready for bed. Going to sleep.

Telling myself that, when we open the door in the morning and blink in fresh sunlight, we will face only the usual. The school bus lumbering up the road, a flash of yellow through dark green pines with its horn honking. Park howling that nobody signed his permission slip for P.E. Then the two little boys running down the driveway to catch the bus, James grabbing a last cup of coffee, winding his tattered scarf around his neck and zipping his coveralls for another day's work in the timber with the screaming chain saw, and me scraping plates into a bowl for the kitten that Park forgot to feed and counting the minutes I need to get myself ready for work. No beast crouching on the roof.

And I imagine what I will say to my sister, days or weeks from now. Do you have any idea how it feels, I will ask her, to lie awake in the dark and know that James, too, is wide awake and listening, although he pretends to be sleeping as quietly as the little boys in their bunks? As the heat of the stoked wood stove fades, do you feel the house gradually cool and creak and settle? Do you hear the child sigh in his sleep in the next room, do you hear the willow twigs scratching to find the chinks between the logs and mortar? Would you be reminding yourself of the measurements of the rafters we sawed, the thickness of the hand-hewn shingles, the wooden skin between ourselves and the wild world?

Can you imagine, I will ask my sister, what it is like to wake suddenly to cold gray light in the window and James's empty side of the bed? To run out in your sweats and bare feet to the *chunk chunk* of wood into the stove and see icicles in James's mustache as he turns from building up the fire and says, "Well, we got an inch of fresh snow last night and a perfect set of cat tracks coming off the roof and headed up toward the north ridge."

Can you imagine, I will ask her, how the mountains might close around Seattle, wrinkling their forests, shrugging the power lines off their shoulders, pouring their muddy floodwater down from the raw sore patches of clear-cut, spilling their scree over the freeways?

Have you seen the lion, my sister will ask, to keep the peace between us.

And then I will tell her about the deer James shot as bait, and the trap he set in the deadfall where the north ridge was logged, long ago, and how, the next morning, the cage of the trap throbbed with a pulse we could feel from the kitchen door.

How the four of us hiked up through the soft snow. How the young female lion looked back at us through the mesh of the cage without apparent fear, with a cat's condescending interest in human doings.

How James handed Park the rifle and asked him if he remembered everything he had been taught.

Ask your law partner, I will say to my sister, if he can imagine being the first in the cold morning to walk out of his Seattle apartment while his wife and little boys sleep. Ask him about walking backward, as James did, into the white light of fresh snowfall, and ask him how the wet flakes felt against his face, upturned for a first glimpse on the overhang of the eaves, of the looming shape, the lightning paw of the beast. Ask him if he would have carried a rifle.

Suzanne, Take Me Down

"She ate all my candy Easter eggs," Ma confides. "All six of them, every one."

Ma sounds so bleak that I turn from stowing her canned groceries on her upper shelves. I turn cautiously, but even then the bench wobbles under me. Ma has this home-carpentered bench which is older than I am and which she uses for a stepstool. I always think that the bench must know Ma, because it has never tipped under her and spilled her on the floor. But one of these days it will break my neck. Fifty-four-year-old man dead in apartment kitchen accident, that will be me.

Then I see that Ma's stiffness is to hold back tears. "What candy are you talking about?" I ask her.

"Oh, Will! When I was in Bonanza last week, I saw candy eggs on special for Easter, chocolate ones with colored frosting, four for a dollar, so I got two dollars' worth, and I gave one to Belle for her Easter present, and one to Mrs. Horn upstairs, and I had six left, which I was saving for little Tabitha. I left them here on the kitchen counter . . ."

"She must have been hungry."

I'm stowing the cans of tomato soup where Ma can reach them when she stands on her bench and hoping I can jolly her out of her mood.

But Ma sounds as sad as if her trust has blown out the window. "Suzanne came in to visit, crying, like she does, and then she said she wanted to get herself a drink of water. I thought she was taking a long time in the kitchen by herself, and after she left I went to look, and here she'd glommed down all six of them decorated eggs. Can you beat that, Will?"

"No, because it makes my teeth hurt to think about it. Don't you think it was a good thing that Suzanne ate all that candy, and not little Tabitha?"

What I can't imagine is anybody stealing food from my mother. Having to steal it. As a boy on the ranch, I'd gotten over being bashful sitting across the table from some sheepherder or rep rider with his elbows on the oilcloth, shoveling down Ma's serviceberry pie. Of course, hospitality was more the custom in those days, and neighboring's a thing of the past, but Ma still limps around this cramped little apartment kitchen and cooks her pot roasts and fried chicken, and she bakes her pies and her hand-whipped angel food cakes for me and Cindy and Tabitha and Belle and Mrs. Horn and anyone else she can persuade to put their feet under her table.

But now this girl, Suzanne.

After weeks of hearing about the runaway Hutterite girl who'd moved into the upstairs apartment back of Mrs. Horn's, I'd only seen her once, in late February.

One of those cold afternoons, early dark. I'd dropped by after work to bring Ma the fresh-range eggs she likes and met Suzanne on the porch steps, on her way out. I knew it had to be her. She was wearing jeans and a jean jacket, and in the porchlight her hair looked reddish and bushy. Just like any girl, early twenties and a little overweight, nothing to show that she used to be a Hutterite. She never even saw me. Of course, to a girl her age, a man my age is invisible.

Now, with the memory of those plump flanks in her new jeans and the bounce in her step as she had headed out through the frost and the shadows of branches that evening, I think of how Suzanne must have crammed Ma's candy Easter eggs into her mouth. Using both hands, gobbling to get them down. Her teeth clogged on marshmallow filling, her eyes furtive on the door. Who could be so hungry for candy?

I finish putting away the groceries and steady myself on the edge of the sink to keep Ma's bench from trying to kill me when I step down.

"Come to think of it, Ma, while you were giving away Easter eggs, why didn't you just give one to Suzanne?"

Instead of looking at me, Ma goes to rubbing at her left shoulder that's given her pain for years, an injury from some wagon accident with horses so long ago that I can't remember a time when seeing her hand slip up to soothe her shoulder was not familiar. For Ma it's a way of stalling, of giving herself a small space, the way reaching for a cigarette creates a space for smokers. I don't think she holds it against Suzanne, but I know that Ma remembers a time when everybody hated the Hutterites for moving down from Canada in colonies and thriving like weeds on good Montana ranchland.

Ma starts to explain, what, I'll never know, because we both hear the bump and scrape at her door, and Belle's toneless bellow.

"Leila? Leila? Are you to home?"

"Come on in, Belle. We're right back here in the kitchen."

Belle whirs through the door in her electric wheelchair, gouging the woodwork with the corner of her footrest and torturing an animal squeal out of her motor before she can find her button for reverse and make a second try at squaring herself around to

Ma's table. No wonder they never can keep paint on the wood-work in this building.

She gives me a sneer. "Will! You again! Don't that fancy wife of yours ever cook for you?"

But her eyes are avid as Ma fills a mug with hot water and stirs in about three parts sugar to one part instant coffee. Her hands tremble when Ma sets it down in front of her. When I was a kid, Belle had an arm that could help hoist a five-hundred-pound hog for butchering. Now here she is, ten years younger than Ma and three times Ma's size, and she can hardly get in and out of that wheelchair by herself. Lives for her sweets.

Ma has poured me a cup of instant, too.

"Should get home," I say as always, but I accept the coffee as always and sit down at my corner of the kitchen table, as far as I can get from the smell of Belle. And oh hell, I don't like myself for letting it bother me. I know she can't drag herself in and out of her bathtub. The truth is that one of these first days, it'll be assisted liv-ing for Belle and another pair of feet missing from under Ma's table.

What's mainly on Belle's mind tonight is Suzanne.

"Last night," she says, glaring at me with her big pale eyes as though she thinks I'm the scoundrel who advises Hutterite girls to leave their colonies for a high life in Fort Maginnis, Mon-tana, "I turned over in bed and looked at my little clock when I seen by the crack under the door when the hall light came on, and sure enough it was three in the morning. Now where could that girl a-been at that hour?"

Ma, who at least got a modern education by raising Cindy for me, shakes her head.

"They've cut her hours back at Bonanza," Belle continues, after she's jiggled her cup up to her mouth, sipped and smacked. "She don't even go to work until eleven. This morning it was a quarter past eleven before she ever left the house. How long do you think it'll take her to get herself fired off of that job?"

I've never figured out how Suzanne can pay her rent, which even for that back apartment has to be three hundred a month, and run her little old car, and still afford to eat on what she earns as a box-out girl, thirty hours a week at Bonanza. And I can't square Ma's and Belle's description of her with the girl I saw that night, bouncing past me with her eyes on the frost halos around the streetlamps. I remember how her footsteps faded on the scraped sidewalk, and how the broken light and shadows absorbed her into the patterns of the snow crystals. She hadn't looked back, she knew where she was going.

"Wonder if she'll go back to the colony for Easter."

"She went back at Christmas," says Ma. "She wanted to see her mother. And do you know what they done? They wouldn't let her eat Christmas dinner in the dining hall with everybody else. She had to eat her dinner in her mother's room, all by herself."

Belle has heard all this before. She sucks her cheeks, enjoying the good out of her coffee and sugar. When she runs her tongue around the rim of her mug, Ma gets up to mix her more.

"She told me, this is the second time she's tried to break away," says Ma. "The other time she tried, she went back."

"Them Hutterites got their ways of doing. Couldn't stomach it, myself. Wearing them black clothes of theirs, and jabbering away. Don't know why anybody'd want to go back to such."

I ought to know better than argue with Belle, but I say it anyway. "Nothing strange in wanting to go home. What's strange is wanting to leave home."

"Why! What are you talking about, Will? With all your book-reading, and you don't know that them Hutterites live just like Communists? They can't own nothing themselves, it all has to belong to the colony."

"If you grew up in the colony, why would you expect to live any different?"

"With them black clothes they have to wear? Skirts down to their ankles and scarves on their heads? And the men! I suppose you'd like to grow a beard and wear a pair of them homemade black trousers, Will!"

Ma gives me that one look of hers. "Suzanne's still got her black dress and her scarf," she says, "and she wears them when she goes out to visit her mother. You bet she does."

Belle is set for a good fight, but I'm ashamed of myself, and I'm overdue at home. I nod good night and let myself out into the dark hall where the old hardwood floors creak and give away Suzanne in the small hours.

The etched glass panel in the front door lets in light from the streetlamp. This was a hell of a house when old Pierre Broussard built it. A mansion, really. That old boy couldn't have known he was installing ornamental sandstone pillars and carved oak doors in a last-stand apartment house for old widows. Or dust for the bulldozers, that'll be next. More cracks open in this house every spring.

On the porch in the dark I breathe the lessening cold and look at the chain of lights down Main Street hill. Old Broussard got a good view of town when he built up here, from the courthouse that holds twenty-seven years of me and is going to hold three more, across the three or four blocks of downtown colored neon and the outlying scatter of porch lights, all the way to the dark slopes and the mute, dark shoulders of the Judith Mountains and the highway where headlights crawl through the gap toward Billings, southeast.

Thirty miles on the other side of the mountains, in the shelter of the buttes, the communal buildings of the Hutterite colony will be winking their lights over snowbound ranchland, and somewhere in that nest of lights, Suzanne's mother will be worrying about her. Either I'm too old to imagine wanting to leave the warmth of the lights, or I'm too young to accept, as Ma does, that it's all temporary.

I can smell the earth in thaw. We're coming into that time of year which I know from the courthouse records, when the old settlers dug graves for the dead that had waited aboveground all the impenetrable winter. Time was when a change in the weather, the smell of a thaw, made me feel horny. Now I only feel the heebie-jeebies waiting in the dark.

Dark clouds speed past half a moon as the wind quickens. I walk down old Broussard's carved sandstone steps and hunch into my coat for the ten-block walk to my house on Yogo Drive.

The old land records are the only part of my job that I'll miss when I retire. There's nothing demanding about what I do, mostly searching and recording land titles, so I don't have much occasion to take down the bound ledgers from the last century. But I like knowing that they're on the shelves behind my desk. I like the yellow leather bindings that creak when I open the pages, and the mottled maroon endpapers, and the legal descriptions of the oldest homestead claims in this county, and the original signatures in real ink.

The oldest recorded plats in the ledgers date from the 1880s, when a man who was free, white, and twenty-one had a right to file a homestead claim on a hundred and sixty acres in the Montana Territory. Pierre Broussard's transactions predate the ledgers by ten years. He wasn't white, he was a mixed blood who came down from the Red River country in two-wheeled carts with his family and two other families and built a log settlement on Castle Creek before there was a town at all.

When I was a boy, I heard Broussard's folks called *breeds*, but they called themselves *metis*. Mixed bloods, French Canadian and Cree for the most part. They'd been wanderers and buffalo hunters almost as wild as the real Cree until they watched the slaughter of the great buffalo herds as the railroads came west, and they knew they needed a place to settle and plant gardens.

Broussard did all right for himself. A lot of the *metis* had their cultivated ground taken from them by white homesteaders, but Broussard hung on to his, somehow. Later he donated land for the hospital and the Catholic church and got his name on a street sign. Dad knew him.

Dad rode into Montana around the turn of this century. His story, which I've never been able to document, was that he was born in Ireland and ran from some trouble, stowed away on a ship to New York, walked to Texas, and signed on to drive the last of the big cattle herds up the old Goodnight Trail while he was still in his teens. He never told the tales I longed to hear, about Indian fighting or cattle rustling, but he did say that he nearly drowned once, when he was fording the flooded Platte by holding on to his swimming horse's tail. Like most cowboys, he couldn't swim.

Montana was still wide open when Dad got here. The gold rush was over, and the Blackfeet had been pushed back on their reservations, and old Broussard and his companions were living in their log cabins along Castle Creek, and a few white settlers had filed land claims. But the big homestead rush hadn't happened yet, and Dad had plenty of elbow room.

He knew Jake Hoover and the young Charlie Russell, and he met some of the famous rodeo hands, like Turk Greenough, and Hoot Gibson, who started in rodeo but later starred in silent films, and he rode with the not-so-famous but locally legendary, like Sid and Farmer Killham. In middle life he met Ma, who was fifteen and lied about her age to get married to him, and together they ran the ranch on Castle Creek until he died in 1959. All this latter part of his story I have documented.

Dad was already fifty when I was born, so I never knew him in his glory days. All I ever got were the stories.

I grew up on the Castle Creek ranch, a sheltered boy in many ways. The only job I've ever been fired from in my life was the summer I was sixteen and working for Belle, mowing hay, and let a good team of horses run into a barbed wire fence and cut themselves to ribbons, which is probably why Belle sneers at me to this day. After that wreck I stopped taking chances. I never got farther away from home than the state college up in Versailles, in Blaine County, where I was studying history and teacher education at the time of Dad's death. I came home then, of course, to help Ma run the ranch. We sold out when I got the county clerk and recorder's job.

Versailles is where I met Cindy's mom. After we were married, she came down and lived with me on the Castle Creek ranch for awhile, and you could say that she made herself a legend, locally, by the time she cleared out. Hard to believe that she's almost as old as I am, wherever she is.

"Tabby, drink your milk," says Cindy. "Grandma, don't worry about her. Suzanne's old enough to look out for herself, which her mother ought to realize."

Ma's kitchen still feels like home to me, although it's sure the hell a long way from the old log house on Castle Creek, and maybe a longer way than that from the house on Yogo Drive where I live with Rose. Ma's same old yellow refrigerator is stuck with pictures of little Tabitha that Rose won't let me keep at home, and the electric light hangs by a cord from the ceiling and reflects on the shiny patches on the oilcloth, and the orange and yellow and green dishes are the ones that used to come as prizes in the Quaker Oats boxes and that collectors pay big money for today.

"I just don't see how she can get along if she gets herself fired from her job," says Ma.

"She's not going to get fired!"

Ma straightens from the oven with her brown pot in her two hands and her face as flushed as a shriveled apple. "Will," she says, "you might as well grab yourself a plate and eat supper with us."

A fragrance of onion and molasses floats off the ham that I know she's layered into her beans, and I shake my head with regret. "Thanks, no, have to get home."

"Shit!"

In the venom of Cindy's voice, I watch Tabitha's face crack in slow motion, like glass being shattered in the aftermath of explosion. I set down my cup.

"Oh, my goodness," says Ma.

"I don't care! He makes me sick! Rose leads him around by a nose ring, and he lets her do it. And she's never even seen Tabitha. Oh, honey. Oh, Tabby, don't howl. Mom can't take it."

Ma sets her pot of beans on the table, lifts the lid. Through the rising steam her face wavers, flesh melting off the bone. "Cindy, help yourself."

"Maybe I should apply at Bonanza. Get a job as a box-out girl. Maybe Rose would like that."

"Your dad ain't saying that," says Ma.

Cindy glares at me through the strands of blond hair that have stuck to her cheeks. "You don't know how it feels to be twenty-five years old and look at the four walls and know that nothing is ever going to change."

"Tabby, Tabby," says Ma. "She ain't going to calm down until you do, honey."

Sobbing, Tabitha holds up her arms to me, and I lift her out of her high chair and carry her, shuddering and damp against my neck, into Ma's front room.

"What kind of a job could I even *get* in this town—"

"Let's look at Grandma's owls," I tell Tabitha.

Ma has plenty of owls, and I show them all to Tabitha, all the owl salt and pepper shakers, and the owl made out of shells glued together, and the picture of the owl upside down on the branch where all the other owls perch right side up. Finally I let her touch the owl Belle made for Ma years ago, out of unspun wool.

"Ow," she agrees.

But I don't move. Next to the aerial photograph of the old ranch buildings is the framed snapshot of Dad in the saddle. The old cowboy on his favorite blaze-faced mare, the familiar thrust of his shoulders, the jut of his boots through the stirrups. He glares at me from under the slant of his hat as though he wonders who the hell I am.

"Dad," says Cindy from the kitchen door, "Grandma says, come and have a plate of beans with us."

Ma waits at the table, rubbing her left shoulder. "Now don't let your food get cold."

"I don't have the patience to cook," says Cindy. "I've got all that commodities cheese. I wonder how cheese and beans would go."

"I'd grate it up in my hamburger casserole," says Ma.

Cindy sounds plugged up from crying. "I don't know why they keep giving me cheese. I can't even give it away. If they caught me giving away commodities, they'd kick me out of the program so fast—"

Ma gives me that one look as though she thinks I might start shouting Rose's speech about unwed mothers on welfare. "It don't make sense," she says, and listens. "Now, who's that knocking on my door at mealtime?"

I get up from my chair and go to see. Waiting in the ill-lit hallway, twisting her hands, is little Mrs. Horn.

"Will?" she whispers, peering up at me through her thick glasses. "Is that you? Is your mother home?"

"Yes, ma'am."

"We were just setting down to table, Mrs. Horn," says Ma from the kitchen door with her green potholder. "Won't you set down with us?"

Mrs. Horn's nostrils quiver at the rich aroma of beans and onions. Under all those sagging sweaters and petticoats she can't weigh eighty pounds, and I could swear she goes hungry half the time. All she has is her little pension. But she never falters. Once a schoolteacher, always a schoolteacher, I guess.

"I'm so sorry to intrude at mealtime. But something upstairs is very wrong."

I can see Tabitha in the lighted kitchen, framed in the door. She's picking up beans, one by one, from the tray of her highchair and putting them in her mouth. Cindy, so young herself with her smeared eyes and straggling blond hair, leans around her baby to hear what we're saying. Her sulkiness softens to curiosity as she tries to follow the frayed thread of Mrs. Horn's old voice.

"Will, it would ease my mind so much if you would just come upstairs with me and take a look."

"If it's Suzanne you're worried about," Cindy calls, "don't bother. She's all *right*. I could tell you where she's at."

Mrs. Horn just waits in all her clothes, the color of a roll of dust swept out of a corner, and just as wispy. Her eyes, magnified behind her glasses, are focused somewhere behind Cindy, so sad that I almost turn around to see what dire fate lurks over my daughter.

"I never heard Suzanne come in or go out today," says Ma. "Or yesterday either, come to think on it. I wonder if Belle saw her."

Her hand sneaks up to her shoulder, starts to rub.

"Usually I can hear her through the ceiling when she goes to the bathroom," she adds.

And I understand that Suzanne is threatening Ma's and Belle's and Mrs. Horn's last safety net, that unspoken arrangement between them and all the other old widows who have lived and finally died in this apartment building, their tacit promise that they will watch and listen for each other's vital signs. They all will be found dead in their beds one day, but at least they will not lie unmissed for days or weeks, they will be found, and by one of themselves. Now they either have to open the net to contain Suzanne or stop trusting it for themselves.

The stairs are old Broussard's handiwork, solid oak and full of dust in the curlicues and crevices. Over the landing, thin sunshine through a stained glass window casts down patterns of red and blue and green leaves and flowers, while the air grows increasingly stuffy, so stuffy that I wonder how anybody lives up here. Outside the window, branches toss and scrape against the shingles in a chinook wind. It's getting warmer outside. Going to be a warm Easter.

The women have followed me. Mrs. Horn, hanging on to the banister and taking the stairs one at a time, like an ancient child, and Ma, who except for her bum shoulder and her bum ankle is agile as ever, and Cindy, carrying Tabitha on her hip and muttering about people who never learn when girls are old enough to take care of *themselves*. Even Belle has sensed the commotion and rolled herself out to see what's going on. Now she waits in her wheelchair at the foot of the stairs and stares up at us with big apprehensive eyes.

I knock on Suzanne's door, and there's no answer. As I listen, once or twice I think I hear footsteps inside her apartment, and then I decide it's either my imagination or the wind rattling the shingles. I knock again, and no answer.

Something about the silence and the upturned faces of the women below me on the stairs wakens the heebie-jeebies in me. I could go back to Ma's apartment, use her phone to call the manager, but tell him what? He's a young fellow, hired by the bank, never comes near the place.

So I try the door, and it swings silently open.

Nothing is behind it. Nothing much. Only the one room, an unmade bed of sorts on the fold-out couch, a tangle of a sheet and a blanket half on the floor. An ashtray full of cigarette butts. Flies crawling around the sink and under burger wrappers and into empty pizza boxes and glasses of curdled stuff.

I open the door to the bathroom, close it when the stink hits me in the face.

"Phew!" says Ma. "Don't they use flush plumbing out at the colony?"

Behind the bed is a closet with a blue-and-white plastic curtain hanging over the door. When I push the curtain back, I nearly jump out of my skin and then feel ashamed that I've exposed my heebie-jeebies in front of Ma and Cindy and Mrs. Horn. What for less than a heartbeat looked like the shadow of a hanged woman is nothing but Suzanne's black dress, hanging from a nail.

On the floor under the dress, a pair of heavy black shoes with laces.

"Leastways we know she didn't go back to the colony, else she'd worn her black dress," says Ma.

"If anybody would *listen* to me," says Cindy from the doorway, "I could tell them that she's been going out with Jake LeTellier, and that she probably partied with him over the weekend and she didn't *bother* coming home."

I turn to Mrs. Horn, to tell her gently that I think Cindy's right, and that Suzanne is somewhere sleeping off the night before, and that we've done all we can, and that she should come downstairs with us and have dinner with Ma. But Mrs. Horn has tottered over to the closet to peer at its contents. I watch as her frail old hand steals out and touches the fabric of Suzanne's black dress. In the most furtive of movements, she lifts the skirt, gives it the smallest shake of life.

And for a moment I see what Mrs. Horn sees. Hadn't I wanted to follow Suzanne that night, away from this stale tail end of living and into the spinning halos of frost? Hadn't I wanted to turn and run after the bounce in her step, the reminiscence in her smile?

Mrs. Horn catches me watching her. Drops the skirt as though it were hot.

"I should very much like to dine with your mother, Will," she murmurs, and condescends to accept my arm on the way down the stairs.

* * *

I tell myself that after I retire, I'll write a history of Murray County, based on the records in the old courthouse ledgers. It will account for all the ghosts. The shadows of Blackfeet warriors on their way over these mountains to raid the horse herds of the Crow. Old Pierre Broussard and his *metis* companions, like flickers of a silent film, cutting logs for their cottonwood cabins and planting their apple orchards. Clouds rolling through sky as Dad rides into the basin on his hotblood mare and notes the timber and high grass and water for cattle. Maybe even the Hutterites, scurrying down from Canada after World War II and settling like ants to build their colonies.

But the ledgers record land transactions, not glorious stories. The land transactions silently show how the Blackfeet saw their territory halved and halved again. How westering whites, entitled by law and by the color of their skins, took homesteads away from *metis* ranchers. How many of those whites lost that same land during the drought years of the twenties and thirties and drifted away, defeated. And how the tough and courageous, like Ma and Dad, who hung on until the fifties, either died or lived to see their land pass into the hands of sons like me.

The newer ledgers record the transactions of widows like Ma and Belle when they sold their ranches and moved to town, and the dates when the fine old houses were converted into apartments for those widows and others, like Mrs. Horn, who never owned land but taught at the county high school for years and told me, when I was a student in her senior class, that brains counted as much as strong backs, and that I should go away and study history.

In the current ledgers I can document the purchase, with my share of the Castle Creek ranch money, of this house of glass and cedar on Yogo Drive where I live with my second wife, Rose.

On the other side of sleep I have been walking along Castle Creek, over frozen mud, as the willows turn yellow after their long dormant winter. The creek is flooded over its banks with snowmelt, threatening to sweep me off with broken, bobbing branches and bunches of grass and weeds, streaming like the hair of the dead, and then the telephone is ringing, and I am awake, and I snatch the bedside phone off the hook before it can wake Rose.

"Will?"

"Ma!"

Trailing the long cord, I carry the phone into the bathroom and shut the door behind me. "What's wrong, Ma? Do you know what time it is?"

"Will, we're just not easy in our minds."

"For God's sake. Not Suzanne again. It's past three in the morning."

But she pours out her story. How they all had been awakened, Ma and Belle and Mrs. Horn, by the screams from the porch. How, in their separate apartments in the dark, they had lain in their beds and listened to the man's enraged bawl, the girl's pleas and sobs. Then his truck roaring away, then the front door opening and closing, then Suzanne crying alone on the stairs.

"But in a few minutes we heard her running back downstairs again," says Ma, "and she ran out the door. And we went in her room and looked, Miz Horn and me, and her black dress is gone from its hook."

"She probably went back to the colony. Did you look to see if her car was gone?"

"It still sets out there by the curb. She ain't bought gas for it for a month."

Through the crack in the bathroom door left by the phone cord, I can see the dim bed and the outline of Rose's arm thrown back over her head in sleep. "It was just a fight with her boyfriend, Ma. Forget it. Tomorrow is Easter Sunday."

"We just thought, Miz Horn and Belle and me, that mebbe you could go and see what Jake has to say. Whether he knows if she's all right. You know Jake LeTellier, don't you, Will?"

"Yes, I know him. Call the police."

Rose moves in her sleep and mutters, and I cover the receiver with my hand, as though from twenty feet away she might recognize Ma's voice on the line. My dream is coming back. I had been walking by water. Water lapped over my boots, sang a fragment of folksong, *Suzanne take me down, to the water's edge,* only those few words with no beginning or end. It's past three in the morning, and I am a fifty-four-year-old county clerk with a song lyric stuck in his head.

"When she goes home to the colony, Will, none of the other Hutterites will talk to her, and her mother cries and tells her that she's going to hell when she dies."

"If she's running around with Jake LeTellier, her mother might be right."

"Just think if it was Cindy."

"Will?" comes drowsy from the bed.

When I carry the phone out of the bathroom, Rose is sitting cross-legged in bed and fumbling for her cigarettes. "Who the hell was that? Wasn't Cindy, was it?"

"No."

"Had to be your mother, then. What'd you tell her?"

"To get some sleep."

Rose yawns so hugely that I can see her ring of teeth and the shadow at the back of her mouth. "God, the awful taste of these things," she says. "Bring me a shot of juice, will you?"

"Sure."

I pad down the hall to the kitchen and turn on the light. Rose's kitchen springs to life in reverse behind the darkened glass of the sliding doors. Oak and tiles and copper and a long-faced man in pajamas who meets my eyes only until he realizes who he is looking at. He turns away when I do and opens his ghostly refrigerator.

I wonder if Rose wants a shot of vodka in her orange juice and decide to chance it that she doesn't. Carrying the glass of juice, I pad back into the bedroom.

But Rose is already asleep.

I set down the glass of orange juice and lift the cigarette out of her hand and stub it out, and I silently gather up my clothes and walk back through the darkened house. As long as the lights are off, the windows will stay windows, not mirrors, and I can look out, suspended as I am over the steep pitch of Yogo Drive in this box of glass and cedar, this dream house of Rose's, where the neighbors are accountants and attorneys, and the trees wring themselves in the wind along the line of streetlamps, all the way down the hill.

Of what I am about to do, I am afraid. I am a fifty-four-year-old county clerk with a second wife and a daughter by a first wife, each of whom tells me that I do too much for the other one and not enough for her. What I will do now is for myself. I reach for my boots and listen to the chinook wind as it carries warm air out of the west at sixty miles an hour, melting the snow in the mountains, flooding the creeks and raising the last of the frost out of the ground so that we dead, who have been kept aboveground for years of winters, will thaw at last.

* * *

I've known Jake LeTellier for years. He was several years behind me in school, right here in Fort Maginnis. Like so many of the fourth and fifth generation *metis,* he was a hell of a good hand with a horse. Rodeoed for a few years, saddle bronc riding. Drifted up to Versailles while I was going to college there, got his commercial pilot's license, finally crashed his plane and got banged up pretty bad. After I came home to settle up the Castle Creek ranch, I heard that he'd been in some kind of shooting incident, had half his stomach shot away. A few years ago he turned up here in Fort Maginnis, and by then he was hitting the booze pretty bad. He shows the not-quite-Indian in his face.

He didn't say much when I knocked on the door of his trailer, just started to pull on his pants.

Stupid bitch, said she was going to jump off the Castle Creek bridge. Hell yes, I'll go with you, but I still ain't going to marry her.

Now we park my car on the shoulder of the Billings highway, just before dawn. The lights of town seem to dance below us as he and I climb out and walk across the asphalt, duck between barbed wires and cut a trail through sodden grass down to the rising edge of the current.

Castle Creek roars like a freight train out of its concrete viaduct. It crashes against the bridge, it chokes the pilings with streams of grass and weeds like heads of silver hair in the quickening gray light.

"What's that over there?" says Jake.

Wrecked cars line the far side of Castle Creek for a stretch of fifty yards below the bridge, hauled there long ago for riprap and left to rust with their glassless headlights looking out like blind eyes over the tumultuous water. Something twists in the current, caught on a fender, long black cloth streaming wet.

Jake and I confer in shouts over the roar of the water.

"How're we going to reach her from here?"

"We'll have to take a chance, cross the bridge before it gets bashed out by them tree limbs, then wade out after her."

"Is she alive?"

"Can't tell. Can you swim?"

"No, can you?"

"No."

Even the old wrecks seem afloat in water up to their hoods. Every model you could name, an old Packard, a Model T, even an old Case tractor, a metal graveyard of the past eighty years, faintly lit and lined up like a sightless version of local history along the flood. I step on the fender of a 1942 Pontiac and feel it dip on me like Ma's treacherous bench, and the next minute I'm thigh-deep in the drench, in a chill more bone-riveting than I ever could have imagined.

Jake grins, flash of teeth. "Did you pee your pants?"

"Yes, damn it."

"Watch out for them tree branches. They could bust loose any time."

That I'm the one to wade into the water after her is a foregone conclusion, because it's Jake who's strong enough to pull us both back out. He leans out as far as he dares from the riprap, grips me by the back of my belt.

· "Wait, let me take just one more step—can you reach her now?"

I can smell the foul eddies behind the line of wrecks, and I feel a drag at my pants leg and a stab of pain from a strand of barbed wire. Hell, Dad, I think. Oh, hell, Ma.

And then I see the girl's face at the brink, the shine of her teeth and the glitter of life in her eyes. With Jake's arm holding me by my belt, I tear loose from the barbed wire, cloth and flesh, and reach for the girl and feel her cold arm around my neck. The bad moment is when I rip her skirt free from the jagged fender that saved her and feel the current try to take us both. Her skirt whips away and vanishes as we waver in the balance, Suzanne and I, teetering on the gutted frame of the Pontiac in thundering waist-deep water that numbs as it tugs and punishes and insists. But Jake holds steady to my belt, hauls back until I find my footing in mud and soaked grass and know that I'm still alive.

My teeth are chattering, and her teeth are chattering, and she has wrapped her naked legs around my waist. Jake has taken off his coat and wrapped it around us both. He shouts something over the roar of water and points to the highway, which is lined with vehicles and flashing lights, a mirror in motion of the dead wrecks along the riprap. And he steadies me as we walk across a sheet of water into the red break of day.

Sister Coyote

1

Driving at night across the prairie is a time when exhausted fancy is likely to grow wings and fly. Old charges of lunacy in the moonlight seem likelier when an alternate world, lit with coldness instead of heat, unfurls from both edges of the highway. The skyline is a warning, every shadow ominous. Silver layers the fence posts and barbed wire, color drains from the sagebrush, the stars withdraw. The young woman who hurtles through these miles at night, enclosed in her car, alone with the warmth of the heater, is reassured by the steady scream of the combustion engine. She won't take her eyes away from the tunnel of light opening ahead of her, except to flick back and forth between the dark verges, watching for antelope or wandering cattle that, hypnotized by her headlights, might bolt into the highway in front of her.

If her eyes do wander out of the tunnel of headlights, she'll jerk them back for fear of what she might see, because under the moon is where the wild things wait. It would be so easy to let her mind go. So easy to slip out from under the weight of consciousness, to close the distance between herself and the night, to be released into the colorless illumination of that other world.

2

The young coyote wakes to the gripe of hunger. Words don't exist for the clench of her empty gut, or the smell of herself or the body heat in the lair she's dug under the sandstone rim of the coulee within a quarter mile of the highway. She recognizes the hum of the car in the sense that she's heard it before and is unafraid, because she has experienced no threat from the noise or the speeding hunk of metal unless it stops and emits the putrid human scent with its extended arm and its crack like thunder. Speeding hunk of metal. Putrid human scent. Crack like thunder. None of these constructions can even approximate what is passing through the brain behind the yellow eyes.

An observer, if there were an observer, would see her unfold her nose from her tail, lift her head and listen. Ears as keen as hers would pick out the faraway sounds, the scritching of small animals in the sagebrush—flesh and blood and body heat on the move—the hunting call of the owl from his cottonwood snag above the river, the mindless yapping of a farm dog at the end of his chain. Who knows, in these night sounds the young coyote perhaps perceives a design, of the world in motion and herself moving with it. At the rim of her den, where the earth is packed hard from the comings and goings of her own paws, she stands and listens for the song of her pack.

Cacophony is more like it. From a range of two or three miles, from the crests of eroded hills, rises the shrill shimmer from four or five shadows like herself, although they sound like fifteen or twenty voices in the extremities of anguish. *Aaooh, aaooh.* But tonight the only ears that hear this wild chorus belong to creatures that live beyond the barricades of metaphor, including the farm dog, who barks and rants and prances at the restraint of his chain.

From the bedroom window, shaddup!

What's bothering him?

Who knows, he hears coyotes maybe.

The young coyote leaves the rim of her den and slips into the sagebrush. She follows the faint trace of a pawpat trail that leads down to the bottom of the coulee, where a thread of water trickles out of a spring that dries up every summer but reemerges in the cool of September and revives a cluster of chokecherries and quaking aspen in time for the first killing frost. Even now, in late snowless December, the stream hasn't quite frozen over, and the young coyote laps water, raises her head with her muzzle dripping, and listens. She stands a scant two feet at the shoulders and weighs less than thirty pounds, although the luxurious fall growth of her coat and ruff makes her look more substantial. Skinned of her pelt, she would make a surprisingly meager carcass of bone and gristle and sheer muscle. But such concerns never infiltrate her consciousness. She trots up the trail to the far edge of the coulee, stops to scratch at fleas—fur, flesh, and intestinal tract, she is a traveling microcosm for fleas, lice, ticks, and worms—and enters the multitudinous shadows of sagebrush.

3

Above the black tracing of cottonwood branches and the shadowy rooftops that descend to the river, the sky hangs grievous and full of snow. It's not quite five o'clock in the old railroad town of Versailles, pronounced Ver-sails, but already dark at this high latitude, only thirty miles from the Canadian border. Headlights soon will be streaming home through the nightfall of late December, but for now the first weakened glow of streetlights casts empty circles on pavement and reflects upward on the portentous weight of the impenetrable cloud cover.

Beth Anne Vanago has just slipped on the outside flight of frozen stairs leading down from her apartment and barely saved herself by hanging on to the precarious banister. Beth Anne's car sits parked in front of her landlady's house in a blanket of frost crystals because she forgot to run an extension cord out of her upstairs window and plug in its headbolt heater last night. Therefore Beth Anne walks right past the car, as fast as she can, with her hands doubled up in her coat pockets.

She heads in no particular direction, but after fifteen minutes with the subzero air searing her lungs, she finds herself on the corner of Montana Avenue and Third Street where her ex-boyfriend Raymond's parents live. Before she can stop herself, she's standing across the street from the narrow frame house with the flaky yellow siding and the little built-on entryway and the light making a pale rectangle of the kitchen window. She shivers, stamping her feet on the bare sidewalk, and tries to decide. She could walk downtown and buy herself a cup of coffee, or she could walk back up the hill to her empty apartment.

But the light draws her. After all, she and Raymond are still good friends, if ex-lovers. No reason why she shouldn't drop in on her way downtown and visit with his mother.

She walks quickly past the two dark humps that are old overshoes that somebody long ago abandoned by the front walk, feels her way through the junk stacked in the entryway, and raps on the door.

Raymond's mother peers out. She doesn't change expression when she sees Beth Anne, just looks out of her tired flat eyes that never reveal her thoughts or reflect the wild times that often wash and break around her.

"Hi," says Beth Anne. Her teeth are chattering. "I was on my way downtown and thought you wouldn't mind if I stopped in and got warm."

She can't tell if there is surprise in the eroded face, but Raymond's mother lets her pass into the kitchen. The rush of warmth from the wood-burning range is downright painful. Beth Anne's fingers tingle as they return to life. Her nose runs. Raymond's mother has returned to the stove, stands stirring with her back turned. From the smell, they're having canned spaghetti for supper. The coffeepot is in its place at the back of the stove, but Raymond's mother doesn't offer her a cup, and Beth Anne feels uncomfortable at rinsing out a cup and helping herself the way she'd learned during the month she had gone out with Raymond.

She hesitates, wondering what to say. Nothing in this airless kitchen has changed, from the sacks of empty tin cans by the sink, to Raymond's posters of Wounded Knee and the AIM manifesto, to the chains of red and green paper the kids had been hanging for Christmas the last time she was here. And yet it's different.

The kids must still be out somewhere, because the house is quiet except for the faint noise of the TV. Beth Anne goes to the door of the darkened front room and sees the flickering square of illumination and Raymond's father rising from the depths of the double bed.

"Hi," she says.

"Well, hi there!"

He climbs out of bed and limps back and forth in his long underwear to clear off a chair for her.

Beth Anne sits down without leaning back and looks at the TV. A game show is on, the host leers out of the screen to the hysterical approval of his studio audience. Should she unbutton her coat? The dark little room is so stuffy.

"So," says Raymond's father. "Are you still the big college girl?"

Beth Anne looks quickly at him, wondering if he is making fun of her weight, but she can read nothing in his bright dark eyes. Philip Juneau is the name he goes by, but she knows it's only the name his Cree grandmother took from the white man she had been living with before she crossed the Canadian border into Montana, years ago. Raymond had told her that a lot of the family still lived up in Red Deer.

"College gets out this week," she says. "It's Christmas vacation."

"Christmas vacation."

"I was really ready for a vacation," she rattles. "I'm not used to being in school again. It's been eight years."

He nods, sagely.

"And the kids to take care of. It's been a challenge."

"Sure."

"I hope Ray decides to re-enroll," she says. "He has a good mind. He should make the most of it."

"That's what I tell him all the time. He ought to hit the books. BIA, they'll pay his fees." His eyes wander back to the TV, where the war news has come on. The screen has filled with bright jungle colors, then eclipses suddenly to a face that talks earnestly under a camouflaged helmet. Hopes for a cease-fire.

The kitchen door bangs and blows in freezing air, and Beth Anne jumps.

"Them kids, how many times I got to tell them not to be hanging around First Street. I'll take my belt to them!"

The girls are in their early teens. Beth Anne has never seen them wearing anything except blue jeans and blue jean jackets. They are wearing blue jean jackets now, in spite of the cold that flushes their faces. The older girl comes in from the kitchen and changes channels on the TV.

"I was watching that!" her grandfather bellows, but the girl goes back to the kitchen as though she hadn't heard him.

Should she change it back for him? But even as she hesitates, Beth Anne sees that he is now following the police show with as much attention as he gave the news.

"My kids are spending the holidays with their father," she says.

"That so?"

But she can tell that he has lost interest in her.

The girls are quarreling in the kitchen. They are the daughters of Raymond's older sister, who moved to Minneapolis long before Beth Anne ever met Raymond. She knows, because Raymond explained it to her, that the arrangement is a holdover from the old days, before their pride had been shattered by the white man's dole and the white man's whiskey, when Indian families looked after their own.

The younger girl stares through the kitchen door, her eyes inquisitive through her coarse black wings of hair.

"Raymond broke up with you."

Beth Anne smiles at her. "That doesn't mean I can't come over and visit your grandparents."

"He's got a girl from Fort Belknap now."

Beth Anne glances at Raymond's father, but he gives no sign of listening. The girls have always made her nervous. They remind her of the Indian children in the fifth grade who waited at recess to chase her and take her lunch money.

"Well," she says, bunching her coat around her, "I should be going."

The old man's eyes leave the screen and flicker over her, but he does not answer.

"I just stopped by to say hello."

Both girls are watching from the kitchen door.

At the last minute, the old man speaks. "The college girl has to hurry away, eh."

Beth Anne's throat stings. "I'm not sure I'm going back to college," she blurts, although she had not intended to tell anyone, and, in fact, had been unaware until she spoke the words that she has really come to this point.

"That so?"

She steals a look at him, wishing she could explain how at first it had been glamorous, after Pete left her, to think about classes and her own life and to learn about Raymond's heritage by listening to him and his friends over endless cups of coffee in the campus cafeteria, but lately something has gone wrong and she doesn't know what it is.

"It just hasn't worked out," she says around the lump in her throat, but the old man has gone back to his program.

The girls lounge in the doorway. They move back, their eyes bright with curiosity, as Beth Anne picks up her purse to leave.

"I'll tell Raymond you just stopped by to say hello," the old man calls.

The girls grin, and Beth Anne has to lower her eyes and remind herself of the fractures of their growing up. She tries to manage a pleasant smile for Raymond's mother, but the old woman never turns from her cooking as Beth Anne walks fast and faster to the door.

Versailles, like so many of the railroad towns that dot the Montana highline like beads on a string, is named for a great foreign city. Ver-sails. Its downtown streets have been hung with crisscross Christmas lights since the week before Thanksgiving, and the reds and blues and greens reflect on spinning frost crystals like winter mirages. The Canadian storm front has been predicted to move in before morning, and by the time Beth Anne has walked as far as First Street, the first sullen snowflakes are floating down. But meanwhile there's plenty of time before the bars close, and the remodeled Jubilee on First Street, with its new dance floor and its out-of-town band brought in for the holidays, is overflowing and noisy.

Beth Anne pauses on the sidewalk in a throbbing pool of electric red and green and listens to the throb of electric guitars from the depths of the Jubilee. She hates to walk inside a bar by herself, so she looks up and down the street and pretends that she's waiting to meet a friend.

Two fat Cree girls stagger through the colored lights on their way to the Palace Bar across the street. Beth Anne, cowering against the fake stone archway that was part of the recent remodeling, can't tell if they're laughing or shrieking. But the way is clear, and Beth Anne grips her shoulder bag and marches herself through the archway.

She stands on tiptoe, but still she can see only the backs of heads and shoulders and legs through the haze of smoke. A barmaid fights her way through the mob with an empty tray and a handful of bills, but she sidesteps Beth Anne without seeing her. A young man in a black cowboy hat bawls in Beth Anne's ear, but before she can answer him, she realizes that he was yelling at a friend and had not seen her, either.

Worse than the fear of being conspicuous is the old panic at being invisible. She looks wildly through the smoke, reminding herself of the long freezing walk uphill and the stale shell of rooms waiting for her. Then she sees the small round table next to her, with empty glasses and empty chairs. No coats are draped over the chairs or hung behind them, and after a furtive moment spent looking in all directions for previous occupants, Beth Anne dares to sit down, lean her arms on the table, and let out her breath.

The band has just shut down for its fifteen-minute union break. In the comparative quiet, Beth Anne looks around, wishing she could get a drink. From the talk on campus, she knows that the younger women and some of the older ones use the bars as a way of meeting men and maybe picking someone up to go home with. Such casual hunting had shocked her at first. In high school it was the sluts, the ones who dropped out of school and married young and got divorced, who went into the bars alone. They were just asking for it, the senior girls had hissed. Beth Anne knows she isn't in high school any longer, it has been a long eight years, and she too has married young and dropped out and divorced. She knows she isn't asking to be picked up, she's taking charge of her own life. Still she feels panicky.

"—*take the ribbon from your hair*—"

She jerks back as the man sings the line from the jukebox song into her face.

"So? You here all by yourself?"

He drops down into the chair beside her, pressing against her left arm and breast. Beth Anne instinctively flinches, has to remind herself to sit still.

"My name's John."

"Mine's Beth Anne," she whispers.

"What?"

"Beth Anne!" she says loudly over the jukebox and the racket at the bar. She knows from listening to the women joking over coffee in the campus cafeteria that nobody uses last names in the bars.

John hangs his arm around her shoulders. His eyes burn in his pasty face. She can smell his breath. She looks down and sees her hands empty in her lap and knows that she has to start somewhere. She lifts her chin and smiles at John.

"*—take the ribbon from your hair,*" he sings again in his high, sweet tenor. He glances toward the bar and then turns and laughs in Beth Anne's face for no reason that she can see.

"What?" she says.

But he doesn't hear her, he's watching the bar. He wears his hair longish and wavy around his round face, and his mustache droops over the nervous twitch of his mouth. Beth Anne can't tell if he's pasty from lack of sunlight, or because the bar lights have drained the color from his face, or because he's sick. But he's a better-looking man than she would have expected to sit down with her.

Raymond had been intelligent, way ahead of some of the professors, but he had been overweight like Beth Anne, and he had a plump dark face and round glasses that made him look like an overfed hawk. She thinks John looks a little like Paul McCartney on the cover of one of the record albums Pete took with him when he moved to Missoula, and she's glad she's still wearing her long coat, because it disguises her heavy stomach and thighs.

John's face looms close. He plants his mouth on hers. Beth Anne holds on to the edge of the table and feels his lips suck at her tongue.

"What are you so nervous about?" he demands, breaking off the kiss. "Don't you like me, or what?"

"I . . . sure, I like you okay . . ."

"Then talk to me some." He glances over his shoulder at the bar. "I'm jumpy tonight, so talk to me, okay?"

He certainly is jumpy. Beth Anne watches the involuntary twitches of his clean white hands and his coal-fire eyes behind the puffy mask of his face as they roam in search of something she hasn't seen yet.

But maybe she really can talk to him. "How come you're jumpy?" she begins.

"What?" His eyes shoot back to her. "Oh. My wife. I mean, she used to be my wife. She left me."

"Oh," says Beth Anne, widening her eyes to look sympathetic. She stretches her neck out of her coat collar to minimize her double chin.

"I was running this club in San Antonio, Texas? Good deal, had a couple topless dancers, and anyway. She dropped me off at work one night—we'd been together maybe eight months and everything was fine as far as I knew—but when I got home, she'd cleared everything out and left a note. If I wanted to see her again, I could find her in Montana. She was from Montana, see. She wanted me out of the bar business."

"When was this?"

His mouth jerks as though her question were pointless. "Coupla years back. She wants me out of the bar business, see? So I come all the way up north, freeze my ass off, work this or that shitting job, until finally her old man gets me a"—he begins to laugh—"gets me a bartending job. After I'd run my own club, he gets me a bartending job at the roughest goddamn Indian bar in this town. Get it? She wants me out of the bar business, and her old man gets me a bartending job!" He laughs and laughs, while Beth Anne watches.

"And then she got pregnant. On purpose."

Beth Anne blinks at this new direction, but John hardly notices. "Hell, I didn't know. Thought she was probably using something. Listen, she told me she'd been married one other time? Know what her own mother told me? Five goddamn times she'd been married before I came along."

Beth Anne swallows. She feels vaguely guilty about the wife who had gotten pregnant on purpose, that being one of the crimes Pete had accused her of. "Your wife—" she begins, but John is craning his neck to watch someone at the bar.

"What the hell. You got no drink? A brandy ditch okay?" he demands, suddenly. He springs up and disappears as abruptly as he came.

Beth Anne tries to see through the wilderness of bodies to the bar. She wonders if John will come back. He doesn't, but soon the barmaid comes over and slops a glass down in front of her. Ice cubes wash through the pale golden liquid.

"That's on John."

"Thank him," says Beth Anne, but the barmaid is already swaggering hard and contemptuously through the crowd of revelers.

She takes a cautious sip of brandy and water. She has never liked the taste of liquor, but she's found that getting past the first swallow helps. She reviews the encounter with John, trying to see it from one point of view and then another, trying to understand what she said that was wrong.

She looks at the Budweiser clock over the bar, she's startled to see how late it's getting. Another drink arrives, the empty glass is swept away. The band is playing again. In fact, they're getting ready for another break.

"—take the ribbon from your hair!"

John has returned so unexpectedly that Beth Anne squeaks with surprise and almost upsets her glass with the involuntary flutter of her hand.

John has brought her another drink. He sets his own fresh drink on the table and sprawls into the chair next to hers. This time his hand on her breast is so insistent that she can feel it through her coat, and she has to tell herself to sit still.

"Listen," says John, leaning toward her until she can't keep his face in focus. "Let's you and me get a bottle of Strawberry Hill and go someplace and celebrate."

"Celebrate?"

But then she realizes that he only means he will share the wine with her before he takes her to bed. She tries to think how to say yes to someone who does not seem to be talking to her, but to some girl he has mistaken her for, or to some girl who exists in another time or perhaps only in his head, and how to say yes before he changes his mind. But already she's too late.

Splat in the center of the table is slapped another glass. Beth Anne tips her head back to look into the angry red face of a woman whose thighs and stomach are nearly as heavy as hers, but who stands six feet tall and looks taller because of the elaborate arrangement of her brittle hair, like a haystack, on top of her head.

"Pleased I met you!" snaps this woman to Beth Anne. She turns to John. Beth Anne watches in fascination as the big haystack woman picks up John's drink and pours it on the linoleum between his feet. Ice cubes rattle on the floor, and people turn around to look.

"You don't hang up on me, turd! Not when I call you! I'll do my own hanging up!"

"Cut it out," says John. "What's the matter with you?"

Beth Anne senses that the crowd has thinned. The band seems to have closed down for the night, and the hardy drunks left at the scattered tables are staring at her and John and the big haystack woman. The young man in the black cowboy hat says something to the barmaid, but the barmaid shrugs. She's found time to light a cigarette, and now she leans on the cash register and smokes, bored.

The haystack woman wheels on Beth Anne. "Pleased I met you!" she repeats.

It dawns on Beth Anne that she's being told to leave. But John has rallied. His white fingers clamp on the haystack woman's forearm and force her down into the next chair.

"What's the matter with you, hah? You pop another diet pill? Why don't you pop another diet pill!"

"You're hurting me," she pleads.

"Hurting you, hah? You shoulda thought of that before you came over here, acting like a crazy woman."

His fingers bear down, and the big woman whimpers. Beth Anne watches, astonished, as aggressor and victim change places before her eyes. When John twists the big woman's arm, she howls in pain.

"Where you been, hah? Out with Mike?"

"No! Just over to the Palace with a lot of people—"

"A lot of people like Mike?"

Beth Anne jumps, her hands fluttering, as the barmaid deals out paper cups and empties their glasses. "Come on, guys, we're closing. Take your go-cups and get outta here."

Beth Anne looks at John, but he's glaring at the haystack woman as she cries through her makeup.

"I never went out with Mike, honest, John, you know that, John, ow—please!"

The barmaid lifts Beth Anne by her elbow. Hampered by her heavy coat and the entangling strap of her purse, Beth Anne struggles, but the barmaid only gazes out of the green triangles of her eyes as she steers Beth Anne to the door.

"You don't want to get drunk with John and the Haystack," she says. "Trust me."

Beth Anne tries to explain that she isn't drunk, she had only drunk the one brandy ditch John had bought her—no, two, three—but crowds and noise and strange people always confuse her, although it's a problem she's aware of and is working on. She wants to look back and see what John is doing, but the barmaid is making her walk too fast.

In the flicker of red and green Christmas lights over the stone archway, the barmaid looks more closely at Beth Anne. "You're Pete Vanago's ex-wife."

"Yes," admits Beth Anne.

"I'll be damned. You ever see Pete anymore?"

"Once in a while. He came to get the kids for Christmas."

"Pete Vanago," says the barmaid. She shakes her head. "Sounds like you can really pick them, honey."

Beth Anne thinks the barmaid looks as lovely as a Christmas ornament, golden and shining in the glow of lights, but as slim and tough as one of the Juneau granddaughters. She imagines that the barmaid is the kind of woman who understands the intentions of men and chooses the ones she wants.

The barmaid finds a hidden switch by the door. The colored lights disappear, and now the streetlights cast patches of weak illumination over what had been bare concrete but is now a bed of fresh snow, an inch deep and unmarked by tire tracks or human footprints. More snow is falling in a thickening curtain.

"Good night," says the barmaid.

Beth Anne stands by herself on the sidewalk under the dead neon. She listens up and down First Street to the jeers and snatches of laughter from people who are leaving the bars and tracking through the fresh snow, probably on their way to breakfast out at the all-night restaurant on Highway 2. Beth Anne thinks about going to breakfast by herself.

She wonders if Raymond really has a girl from Fort Belknap. Possibly the little girl made up the whole story to see how Beth Anne would react. If there's a chance that Raymond still cares about her, a chance that her telephone might be ringing in her empty apartment right now—maybe even Pete—but she stifles the wish the moment she's aware of it. It's bad luck to hope. But she can go home and wait. Burrowing her head into her coat collar, thrusting her hands deep into her coat pockets, Beth Anne trudges under the streetlights, into the falling curtain of snow.

4

Through a maze of sagebrush, the young coyote follows an invisible path that veers within a hundred yards of the highway before it angles north toward a moonlit butte. Another thirty miles and she would be crossing the border between Montana and Alberta, Canada, not that she cares or that she has ever traveled so far. Her hunting ground is an approximate five square miles around an old den where she was born eighteen months ago. When her path dips under a barbed wire fence, her back hairs just brush the barbs on the bottom wire, and she shudders. Not because the fence is unfamiliar, its warped cedar posts and singing metal have stood in a straight line through her shape-changing territory for countless of her generations, but because it is a part of that other world, that transparent map of lines and grids laid over her own, that attracts and repels her.

At the base of the butte, other shadows slip out to meet her shadow. Much dancing follows, much sniffing under tails. Two of the pack are her remaining littermates, one is a half-grown survivor of a later litter, and one is a scrawny veteran of her mother's generation, or perhaps even her grandmother's. The young coyote is the dominant female, she's already reached the average lifespan of her kind. If she lives through the winter, she'll give birth to five or six pups and rear two or three through the following summer, and she may see one or two reach adulthood. Starvation, traps, poison, bullets, or being ripped apart by packs of hunting hounds, these are the ordinary fates. None of the denizens of the moonlit world die of old age.

And yet the observer from the realm of language, if there were an observer, would surely gloss the pack's behavior with words like *zest*. Surely these yellow-eyed bundles of bone and stringy muscle are in love with their bodies and with each other's bodies as they frisk and prance and sniff and finally trot off together through the sage and bunchgrass, absolutely unencumbered in a freedom beyond human imagining.

Now they trot, as though by some prior agreement, down the slope of the butte, along the ridge, under invisible sky from which snow will soon fall. Five of them, taking full advantage of the slightest shelter, dip of ground or clump of buckbrush or shadow of sage, until anyone who happened to be watching might think that the ridge itself is on the move. And yet, in the spring of their trot and the carriage of their heads and plumed tails is a vigor, yes a *zest*, that suggests not a mere hunting trip, but a quest for *fun*.

5

When the phone does ring, it's as insistent as if it knows she's curled in the familiar sag on the side of the bed that used to be Pete's.

The chance that it's Pete wakes her up enough to fight her way out of the tangle of sheets and feel for the receiver without opening her eyes.

"Hello?"

"Honey?"

Disappointment drags at her, but she manages to unwind the sheets from her legs and sit up. She sucks at the sides of her mouth for enough saliva to unthicken her tongue.

"You weren't still *asleep*, were you?"

"No," lies Beth Anne. She opens her eyes a crack. The light coming through the tie-dyed curtains is the ominous gray of late afternoon, though perhaps it's only the snowstorm making the day dark.

Her mother sighs. "I don't understand how you can just *let go*. Sleeping in the daytime! What are you going to do when classes start again?"

Beth Anne sits heavily in the sag of the bed. College. That was it. She ought to find some aspirin.

"If you could just get rid of some of that *weight*! Wait until you see the clothes we've been getting in."

At the shop. The day before Christmas. Promising to work.

"Have you heard from Pete? When is he bringing the children home?"

"I don't know." Beth Anne holds her head and tries to think. If tomorrow was the day before Christmas, next week must be New Year's Eve. "On New Year's Eve."

A silence. Then her mother says, "I can count on you tomorrow, then."

"Sure."

She doesn't have to tell her mother about her classes right now. No reason to spoil her holidays.

The receiver feels clammy from her palm. Beth Anne sets it down and opens her eyes enough to look around her bedroom. Blue jeans, bra, and panties lie in separate little heaps, marking her trail to bed last night. Hidden behind the knot of her sweater on the dresser is the old prom photograph of herself and Pete, but from the bed she can see the colored school pictures of the two older children, Emily and Peter.

She might as well move. She heaves herself off the bed and staggers, spraddle-legged to cushion her full bladder, over to the dresser. She looks at the alarm clock. Four o'clock. Worse than she thought; she's slept away another day.

"I can understand people sleeping through an eight o'clock class," the professor of the current issues class had said when she finally went to talk to him. "But noon?"

The pictures of Peter and Emily will melt into blobs as bright and pointless as strings of holiday lights if she stares at them long enough. But the black-and-white photograph always remains itself.

Now Beth Anne squints at the girl in pale tulle and the boy in the dinner jacket whose faces are set in grinning rictuses by a hired flashbulb. She had thought she was fat even then, but she hadn't been. She had been tiny. She had worn the lovely dress her mother had ordered through the shop, especially for her, and she had had her hair done in the angel ripples all the high school girls had copied from the girls on television that year.

Now she looks down at a stomach wattled with stretch marks and underpinned by the swollen drumsticks of her thighs. Her bladder burns.

No need to find a housecoat, no one else is in the apartment. No need to bother shutting the bathroom door. From the toilet she can look across the hall and into the other bedroom with its empty crib and green plastic diaper pail, gray sheets and Disney quilt dragging off the bed Peter shares against his will with four-year-old Jeremy. Emily won't sleep in the bedroom with her brothers. The first day in the apartment, she spread her blankets on the living room couch and wouldn't let anyone sit on it. She wanted her own room back. They all did. Only Caroline, the baby, didn't care.

I'll help with the house payments, Beth Anne, if you'll just try not to make so many changes so *soon!* You can help at the shop from time to time—you can set your own hours and have plenty of time for the children and your classes—and you'll meet someone . . .

Get off the pot, Beth Anne reminds herself. She wipes and flushes and slowly follows last night's path to bed, picking up garments and putting them on as she comes to them. Maybe she'll shower tonight. Right now a shower is just too much effort.

When she pulls her door shut and pauses on the landing, looking down over the rooftops, the streetlights have already come on again. Fresh snowfall has buried the gutters and the ruts leading into alleys, obscured the smoke-stained eaves and chimneys, and smothered the trash and the human leavings with its deep white blanket. Far down along the river, Versailles is still ugly, still the same old railroad town with smoke and steam rising from the cinders and oil stench of the railroad yards, with the exhaust of traffic hanging over First Street and the bars and all-night cafes. But from Beth Anne's landing, all is clean snow and branches and stars and dead stillness.

She has forgotten to plug in the car again, but a walk will do her good. When she first got out of bed, she had been certain she never wanted food again, but now her stomach is growling. She stops on the corner of First Street and Alder under a cluster of styrofoam bells and tries to remember how much money she has left. Then she remembers that she's going to work for her mother tomorrow, and that she'll be paid. Hefting her shoulder bag, she crosses the street and heads for the Night Owl Café.

The Night Owl doesn't do much dinner business, and the drunks won't come in for bacon and eggs and coffee until after the bars close. The cook leans his skinny arms on the service window, smokes a cigarette, and watches the narrow plume rise toward the bright kitchen lights. In the warmth and quiet, Beth Anne chooses a booth and slides in. She waits for the waitress, a shrunken woman in pink Dacron, to get up from her coffee and bring a plastic-covered menu and water in a purple plastic glass.

"Know what you're gonna have?"

"No," says Beth Anne. She wants to read the menu.

Next door is the Palace Bar. Over the swinging doors Beth Anne sees the TV above the bar and hears bursts of laughter and the break of balls across the pool table. The only signs of Christmas are the garlands of sharp synthetic evergreen over the door. She shrugs out of her coat and spreads out the menu in front of her. She feels better.

"Don't give me any of that shit, man!"

Beth Anne goes rigid. Several Indians are pushing each other through the swinging doors, crowding into the booth behind her. Raymond and two other men and two women.

The waitress sighs, gets up and brings them menus and water in two purple glasses and three orange glasses.

"I didn't give you no shit, so quit riding me about it, okay?" says the Indian facing Beth Anne. He's a skinny man with stiff shoulder-length hair and wire-rimmed glasses with thick lenses.

"I ain't riding you."

Beth Anne drinks coffee without tasting it. The women's crow's-wing hair and closed faces remind her of the Juneau girls. You ought to feel sorry for those little Indian children. They've got no chance at all, her mother used to tell her when the tough kids from Grant Elementary chased her home with rocks, but Beth Anne always ran.

"Hey!" shouts Raymond. "What's the matter with you guys?"

The crash of a chair sends a wave of coffee over the rim of Beth Anne's cup and into her lap. An ashtray spins across the linoleum. The waitress jumps to her feet, her mouth opening and shutting silently.

"Don't shove me around!"

"I ain't shoving you around!"

But both men are out of the booth, cuffing each other and shouting angrily.

"You guys!" pleads Raymond, trying to get between them. The skinny Indian shoves Raymond, dislodging the Scotch plaid cap that always rides too high on his head. All three lurch against a table, which tips and spills salt and pepper shakers and paper packets of artificial creamer on the floor. The skinny Indian has lost his glasses. Beth Anne realizes that all three are so drunk that they can stay on their feet only with careful concentration, but still they shove and slap at each other.

"Cut it out!" shouts the waitress. Like an ineffectual terrier, she circles and barks orders until the table crashes over with all three men on top of it. The waitress leaps out of the way. She looks for help and sees the barmaid from the Palace watching through the swinging doors. "Call the cops!" she shouts. "I mean it! Really do it!"

One of the Indian women sees her chance and dives in to retrieve the lost glasses. She sits back down, smiling nervously at her friend.

"What's the matter with you guys?" implores Raymond. He sounds as though he seriously wants to know what's the matter with them.

"Just don't shove me around!"

The skinny boy, blinking and soft-eyed without his glasses, suddenly works his mouth and lurches down the tunnel toward the men's room. His antagonist ponders for a long moment, then bellows his name and charges after him.

Raymond starts to follow, then comes back and sits down with the women. "Did you find his glasses?"

The girl nods.

From the depths of the men's room something thumps against a wall. Then several thuds and a crash. The waitress, who had subsided with her coffee, leaps to her feet again as the swinging doors from the Palace open on an enormous man in a shiny dark blue windbreaker and a dark blue cap with a badge and insignia. Another man in dark blue follows right behind him.

"They're in the gents," says the waitress, and the two policemen disappear down the tunnel toward the closed door.

A silence. One of the Indian girls takes a quick sip of water from a plastic glass, one of the orange-colored ones. Then there's another crash and a yelp, and the smaller policeman comes out of the men's room, herding along an Indian whose arms seem unnaturally stiffened in front of him until Beth Anne sees that he's handcuffed. Next comes the skinny Indian, handcuffed and naked-faced without his glasses, and behind him the enormous policeman.

Raymond springs up. "Here's his glasses! Listen! He's gotta get up and go to work tomorrow, or he'll lose his job!"

"You're coming, too," says the enormous policeman.

"Me! I wasn't in on it!" Frantic, Raymond looks around and sees Beth Anne. "All I did was try to keep them apart. Ask her!"

Beth Anne's mouth has gone stiff, but she manages to force it out. "He wasn't in on it."

"Come on!" Raymond begs. "I have a job interview in the morning!"

Beth Anne knows he's probably telling the truth. She had typed several applications for tribal jobs for Raymond the week before they broke up. Trembling, she gets to her feet.

"He didn't do anything except try to break it up," she says, with as much conviction as she can work up.

"You can tell it to the police judge in the morning."

"Listen," says Raymond to Beth Anne. "How much money have you got?"

She tries to remember. "Three dollars—no, wait, three seventy-five."

"Shit. Okay, listen. Go and tell the old man what happened. Tell him it'll be fifty dollars bail, maybe even a hundred, but he's got to spring me tonight, because I talked to Joe Peppy yesterday and the job's mine if I can just get to the goddamn interview—"

"Let's go, let's go!"

"Tell him! Remember! I talked to Joe Peppy!"

"Okay," Beth Anne promises.

"You two clear outa here," says the waitress. Hands on her hips, she stands over the two Indian women who, eyes lowered, gather their purses and gloves, zip their parkas and tie their scarves. They take their time at it.

Beth Anne sits back down. Her hamburger waits on its white restaurant plate, congealing in its grease. Her mouth feels so dry that she doesn't think she can swallow, but she thinks it would be a good idea to act as naturally as she possibly can, so she takes a bite of hamburger and wools it around in her mouth.

"Were you with them guys?"

"No."

When she gets up to pay, the waitress snatches her ticket and slaps it down on the spindle. "Them goddamn troublemakers," she says, punching the keys of the cash register as if she's trying to break them. "Come in here spending taxpayers' money on booze. Them goddamn ki-yis."

Beth Anne trudges along Montana Avenue through a foot of unshoveled snow, dreading her task. But after all, Raymond's father has a right to know what happened. The arrest had been unfair, as Beth Anne can testify. He might choose to make an issue of it.

But when she knocks, Raymond's mother comes to the door and looks out at her without changing expression.

"I have to talk to Ray's father! It's important!"

One of the girls crowds up behind her grandmother. "Who is it?"

"Wait!" Beth Anne cries in desperation, because Raymond's mother is closing the door. "Ray's in jail!"

She had not meant to break it to his mother so crudely. The old woman, however, seems unmoved.

"Ray's in jail?" pipes up the little girl, bright-eyed.

"Yes, and I have to tell your grandfather so he can bail him out."

"He won't bail him out."

"But he's got to! Ray has a job interview in the morning. He's already talked to Joe Peppy. Tell him the bail's going to be fifty dollars, or maybe even a hundred—"

Raymond's mother speaks for the first time. "You take yourself off," she said in the heavily accented English that most of the older Crees spoke. "Raymond, he don't want you."

The door shuts.

The main thing is not to cry. She tells herself that. She stands in the frigid entryway, willing back the tears until her eyes adjust to the dark and she can see the white lines where snow has sifted through the cracks in the siding and spread like fingers across the uneven floor. She gives one last look at the light in the Juneau kitchen. Raymond's mother must not have understood her. Beth Anne knows that her English isn't very good.

It's a relief to get back on a public sidewalk, but her feet are aching by the time she reaches the police station, climbs the steps, and opens the door under the globe light. What looks like a discarded church pew takes up half of the tiled foyer. A place for the public to sit and wait, she supposes. The pew faces a glass barricade and a wall clock that points to nearly eleven. Behind the barricade a young man in a black cowboy hat leans against a desk, drinking coffee out of a styrofoam cup and talking to the dispatcher.

The dispatcher, a young woman in uniform and headset, glances around, sees Beth Anne, and wheels her desk chair closer to the speaker hole in the glass.

"What can we do for you?"

"I have to see Raymond Juneau."

"Who?"

"He's one of them that Mike brought in," says the man in the black hat.

The dispatcher studies Beth Anne. She looks Indian herself, with her flat black eyes and lacquered black hair under the wire bows of her headset.

"What do you want to see him for?"

Beth Anne's eyes and nose are running from the sudden heat. She digs for a tissue in her coat pocket, just in time. "He asked me to tell his father he was in jail," she says, when she can trust her voice. "About bail. But his family wouldn't even—"

"Look, honey, why don't you just go home? He'll have to appear in police court in the morning anyway. A night in jail won't hurt him. Let him sleep it off."

"But his job! He has an interview in the morning that he's waited a long time for—"

The dispatcher exchanges glances with the man in the black hat. Then she shakes her head. "Go home, honey," she said. "Just go home."

* * *

Outside the police station, the globe light shines through freshly falling snow. Another storm has blown down from Canada. Beth Anne finds herself wandering through a haze of snowflakes toward the Jubilee. Maybe it will snow all night. She desperately doesn't want to go home. But where?

"So? You all by yourself again?"

It takes her a full minute to recognize John from the Jubilee. John's eyes explore her face, inquisitive.

"So, you want to go someplace for a drink?"

Something about John, something John has done, ought to make her walk away, but Beth Anne can't remember what it was. Her legs ache with cold and fatigue. She feels as though she has been walking on concrete sidewalks all her life.

"I guess so," she says, and falls in step with him.

6

In her car, driving in the pure light of the coming snowfall, the young woman feels the call of the dog and wolf in her bones and tries to imagine a total and unencumbered freedom. She would grow fur, she would trot off through the sagebrush in the cold light. She would learn to distinguish every blade of shortgrass, to hear the scratch of her toenails on frozen alkali, to follow the smell of blood from miles away.

7

"Turn over on your belly," John tells her.

"What?"

"Turn over on your belly. I don't like to have to look at them when I fuck."

Beth Anne's head is fuzzy with Strawberry Hill, but obediently she wallows over on the bed with the sheets bunched under her. Dimly she feels John pulling her knees apart.

"You're fatter'n a goddamn sow."

A part of her mind swims up through the wine fog to warn her that hurting her with words is not his only purpose. He's beginning to breathe hard. She hears his pants, weighted with belt buckle and small change, as they hit the floor. The foot of the bed creaks with his weight.

"Stick your butt up, wouldja."

Beth Anne walks her knees up under her until she feels herself suck in air. John is wheezing behind her. Then a finger explores her, poking hard once or twice. The finger pulls out, and Beth Anne, her own fingers clenching the sheets, hears the slap slap of flesh on flesh as he thrusts against her. She jiggles with the onslaught, but the one thing she's clear about, through the wine fog, and that's the soft bud of his penis between the cracks of her butt.

"Oh, shit," says John from miles away. The bedsprings creak as he steps off onto the floor. Beth Anne hears him pick up his pants from the floor and wonders if he's going to get dressed and go home. Then it dawns on her that he's pulling his belt out of the pant loops.

She lets out one howl with the first lightning crack of the belt across her butt, but even through the red pain and astonishment she remembers the thin walls and the landlady downstairs, and she chokes off the next howl by biting into the Dacron pillow. The Dacron swells and fills her mouth as she bucks up and down, trying to get out from under the pain. The brightly lighted walls and dresses swim past her, topsy-turvy.

She knows that John is mounting her, because she can no longer move freely. His thing is hard now, no problem. It's making an insistent space for itself inside her. In and out. A relentless thump thump and he's done.

John rolls over on his back with his eyes shut. "God," he laughs, "that was good."

Beth Anne works the pillow out of her mouth with her tongue. The pain has cleared her head even as it subsides to a dull burn.

"Whatsa matter," he gasps without opening his eyes. "Didn't you come?"

She raises herself on one elbow and looks at him, trying to believe that he means what he seems to mean. John cracks one eye open to see why she hasn't answered.

"I just never feel much that way," she gabbles hastily, but that explanation sounds so crazy, even to her, that she adds, "I mean, on my stomach it's the wrong angle or something—"

John yawns. "Roll over on your back and I'll do something nice for you."

Whatever he might take into his head to do next, Beth Anne thinks it wiser to obey. She rearranges herself, wincing as the swollen stripes across her buttocks brush against the rumpled sheets. She squints against the overhead light as John, propped on one elbow, reaches over with his other hand and explores down into her private hair. His roving fingers find the little hood of flesh, stop, and begin to massage, gently but without ceasing.

Beth Anne knows now what he's doing, not because Pete or Raymond ever did it to her, but because she did it to herself when she was in high school. Her heart begins to pound. At first she thinks it's pounding from fear, but the sane voice in her mind warns her of the gathering sensation in her groin. Her eyes roll back as she feels all her flesh grown heavy, all feeling concentrated under John's relentless fingers.

"Uh. Uh—uh," she hears from her own throat.

"You like that?" asks John, and his voice brings her back long enough to open her eyes and catch a glimpse of him, propped on his elbow and watching her with interest. But her heavy flesh drags her back, she's at the mercy of her inert limbs, she's pulled down by gravity itself.

"Uh—uh—"

Her heart gives a mighty lurch. For just a second she can lie free of her flesh while the blood surges in her throat and the mattress creaks and John goes on rubbing. Then she opens her eyes and turns away, wishing he had stopped sooner.

"Did you come?" asks John. "Knew I could get you to." He sniffs his fingers and rolls over. His breathing thickens and becomes regular almost at once.

Beth Anne lies in the sag that had been Pete's side of the bed, listening as John's breathing turns to snores. John's secretion drains down between her legs, making her itch, and she knows she should get up and go to the bathroom. Carefully, not creaking the bedsprings, she sits up and looks at John where he lies on his back with his mustache feathering out with every breath. He's still wearing his cowboy shirt, soft white muslin with a blue flowered yoke, and beneath it his thin bare legs look ridiculous. Stone sober, Beth Anne inventories his tender white shanks, his soft abdomen, and his mottled red genitals like a growth in a nest of dark hair.

Taking care not to jar her sore buttocks or to disturb John, she sidles crabwise to the edge of the bed and onto the cold floor. She inches open the closet door, pulls out the frilled pink nylon housecoat that had been a gift from her mother on her last birthday. She's always felt foolish in pink, but tonight her fingers shake in their haste to drape that filmy disguise over her sagging breasts and the dewlaps of fat that hang over her pelvis.

Strange how willing John had been to give her pleasure once it took no toll from himself, and now he sleeps with his belly exposed and his penis vulnerable. And a fantasy comes uncalled for, vivid as lightning, of herself ripping into that soft white abdomen with something sharp.

Her stomach growls so loudly that she glances to see whether it disturbed John, but he doesn't twitch, so she steals past the bed to the kitchen to see what food she might have left.

In a kitchen drawer she finds most of a loaf of white bread in its plastic wrapper. She carries the bread to the window and sits gingerly down on a kitchen chair. The snow beneath the window reflects a faint oblong of light. Light grows on the rooftops as the dark and snowbound town moves toward dawn. Beth Anne wads the slices of white bread and stuffs them into her mouth. But her mind keeps straggling after a fugitive emotion, like a name forgotten, which she thinks she once has been promised but has never received.

Although once she had come close to having it.

Pete Vanago sprinted down the dirt track with the pole gleaming like a lance before him. He planted the pole and soared up and up, sunburned muscular body and blue jersey and golden head against a blue spring sky before he cleared the bar and fell. Beth Anne jumped up and down, squealing with the other girls who looked at her differently because Pete Vanago was the second best high school pole vaulter in Montana and because Beth Anne Connell had been out with him in his Plymouth Fury the night before. Pete Vanago was a secret weapon in Beth Anne's hand.

Beth Anne shakes the crumbs out of the bread wrapper and licks them off her fingers. Superimposed against the quiet streets and pinpoints of streetlights in the window is the reflection of her own pink-draped bulk. Beth Anne stares into the reflection, but the face stays blank.

8

Seeing the single gleam of light a mile from the highway, with the yard light burning over the indistinct dark lines of outlying sheds and corrals in the shelter of a low bluff, the woman in the hurtling car thinks not of lunacy but of loneliness. Wild animals aren't burdened by self-consciousness, she understands that. Coyotes merge with the folds and crevices and sage-dotted hills, owls fuse with the fence posts they perch on, their small prey waits trembling in ruts and hollows, but how can people bear to live out here?

9

Beth Anne hangs her coat on the hook at the back of the shop and pours herself a cup of coffee in her mother's blue mug. She lowers herself onto the silver-gilt chair that fits her mother's size nine hips and winces.

"Hemorrhoids?" asks Florence, interested.

—*continued cold*, says the radio. *Scattered snow showers late this afternoon and evening.*

Beth Anne takes a deep swallow of coffee and stands up again. She thinks the sharp edges of the chair must have reopened her wounds, because her butt is stinging. She carries her cup through the racks of clothes, across the pale blue plush carpeting, and looks out the window where snow lashes at the lettering, *Beth Anne*, in silver script. Oh honey we'll use Daddy's life insurance money, her mother had breathed. It'll be the Beth Anne Shop. It'll bring us luck.

—another Canadian cold front is expected to bring subzero temperatures and hazardous driving conditions to the state late tonight and tomorrow. Holiday motorists are advised to use extreme caution.

"Look at that wind," Florence says. "With this weather, we'll be lucky to get customers. The day before Christmas! Is your mother coming in this afternoon?"

"I guess."

"A woman might as well make up her mind to it. Once she's past forty, and I don't care what she looks like or how well she keeps herself up, she's expendable. I hope your mother knows that."

"Has she got a new boyfriend?"

Florence rolls her eyes. "And I'll tell you what he likes about her, and it's the same thing that Vanago kid liked about you, and that's her credit rating. Well, we all have to learn."

Her alligator heels sink into the plush as she goes to unlock the front door for business. Beth Anne looks furtively about the shop. With its silver Christmas decorations and its deceptively lit mirrors, it's a hothouse for women, so insulated and overheated that the snow on the street hardly exists.

She stations herself by a rack of party pajamas where she can watch for customers. The few passers-by on the street are bent almost double against the wind and stinging snow. Shivering women and an occasional man stop and gaze at the white and silver window display while, in the rear of the shop, Florence smokes and drums her gold fingernails.

A middle-aged woman wrenches the door open against the wind. A small avalanche of snow falls off her coat as she struggles to see through her fogged glasses.

"May I help you?" asks Beth Anne, with Florence's eyes on her.

"Well, I was kinda thinking about a sweater for my daughter. Maybe a medium. I know you're high-priced."

Beth Anne lifts down boxes containing the picked-over stock of sweaters. She lays several cardigans across the counter. A strand of pink Orlon clings to her finger. Its faint petroleum odor reminds her of the expensive clothes her mother used to bring home to her from the shop.

"Now this is lovely!" Across the floor from Beth Anne, Florence selects a length of black lace and holds it against her own heavily chained bosom. A grizzled rancher stretches a weather-cracked finger toward the lace, draws it back.

"Fifty-nine dollars," he marvels.

"Fifty-nine dollars for this rag," hisses Florence as she comes back to gift wrap the nightgown. "He better hope the price of fat lambs goes up."

Her gold-tipped fingers fly over the embossed silver paper, the tape, the bow. She has passed the blue and silver package over the counter and extracted the rancher's fifty-nine dollars before Beth Anne finishes gift wrapping the pink sweater.

Julie Burchette, who was in Beth Anne's high school graduating class, struggles through the door. She wipes her hair out of her eyes and hesitates by the rack of party clothes. She riffles through the hangers without looking at the size markers.

An arch of Florence's eyebrow sends Beth Anne reluctantly across the plush carpet to meet Julie. "May I help you?"

"Oh—" Julie pulls at a shiny, multicolored leg from a pair of party pajamas, lets it drop. "Actually, I suppose I ought to try something on."

Then she recognizes Beth Anne and stares out of her blue-shadowed sockets. *At least I haven't gained weight!* is as plain as if she had spoken it.

Florence glides in. "Have you seen this ensemble, Julie? I've been keeping it back for you. Oh, Julie, with your hair!"

Julie's hair is pale and ratted away from her small face. The collar of her coat is made of some kind of pale dyed fur, almost the same shade as her hair, and the strands of hair and fur are stuck together with melting droplets of snow.

"A beautiful set, one of our last shipments!"

A young man looks through the shop window, hesitates, then enters. When he walks over to the sale table, Beth Anne sees that he's seriously lame, almost lopsided from a stiffened knee. When he takes off his black cowboy hat and looks for somewhere to brush off the snow, she realizes where she's seen him before.

Two well-scarved women have just fought their way through the wind. Now they're pawing through the costume jewelry. Florence catches Beth Anne's eye and jerks her head in their direction.

"Do these really cost forty dollars?" asks the man in the black cowboy hat. He strokes a dark red sweater.

"Twenty percent off," Beth Anne points out.

He adds and subtracts in his head.

"We were about to mark those down another twenty percent, Jake," calls Florence on her way to the fitting room with her arms full of silver lamé.

He thinks for another minute and digs for his wallet. "Got a cousin would surely be pleased to get a sweater from the Beth Anne Shop," he says.

Clothes from the Beth Anne Shop are famous all over northern Montana. Beth Anne wishes she could smile back at him.

"Seems tight," complains Julie Burchette, emerging from the fitting room.

"Oh Julie, do you *think* so?" cries Florence.

Beth Anne glances back at a Julie multiplied over and over in the triple mirrors. All the Julies are dressed in two-piece evening suits made of silver lamé. All the trousers are slashed in diamond cutouts along the outer seams, and all the cutaway diamonds expose the Julies' gray-white flesh.

"You got them earrings in gold instead of silver?" asks one of the women at the costume jewelry rack.

Florence is reassuring Julie and gift wrapping the dark red sweater for Jake at the same time. Beth Anne knows that they never gift wrap sale merchandise, and she wonders what's gotten into Florence.

"I really need to buy something," Julie admits.

"Here you go, Jake. Merry Christmas. Oh, Julie, what it does for your hair!"

Julie, the original Julie, raises doubtful hands to her damp mop, and so do all the other Julies. The slashed necklines expose the whitish line of their brassieres and the dull blue stretch marks like bites across their breasts.

"Pete and his girlfriend are coming up from Missoula and Bud will want us to go out with them, and I'll *need* something," she says. She looks up, sees Beth Anne, remembers. "Oh," she said. "I didn't mean."

Something more menacing than hunger rouses and snarls in Beth Anne's stomach. Hoping to still it, she walks as far as the snow-driven window and feels the women at the jewelry rack pivoting to watch her. One of them may have called something after her: "Hey! I made up my mind!"

Beth Anne hears the wind. Then she remembers that she cannot hear the wind through the deadening insulation of the plate glass, she can only watch the pattern of blowing snow. She doesn't know what she hears.

From the perfume she knows that Florence is standing behind her. She turns and watches as Florence's brown lips move. Florence's long, gold-tipped fingers clasp Beth Anne's wrist. Reach around your wrist, make your own living, her grandmother told Beth Anne when she was a small child. Florence has been making her own living for a long time. Beth Anne thinks she looks like an aged snake with her rattles coiled and a hide tough enough to skin and tan.

"My coat," she remembers. "I have to get my coat."

She feels herself drawing their eyes out of their sockets. Florence and Julie and the women shoppers, still holding the imitation gold and silver earrings, and the man in the black cowboy hat with his red sale sweater in its expensive blue and silver gift wrapping. She thinks the man in the black hat is about to speak, to intervene, to pity even. But she can't handle pity right now. She wades through the sinking carpet and snatches her coat and shoulder bag from the hook and flees through the back door to the alley. The force of the genuine wind is a relief.

* * *

The wind blows Beth Anne in a flurry of snow across an empty parking lot and two blocks down the street with no more trouble than if she were a dry leaf left over from fall. Along with Beth Anne the wind drives snow and grit, trash and jetsam from the gutters of town. Beth Anne escapes around the lee side of an implement dealership and catches her breath while the wind screams down First Street.

Over the flat roofs Beth Anne sees the line of snowy buttes to the north. Where the cottonwoods still overhang the river current was the site of the old Assiniboine village. Tourists and professors of anthropology still visit the bend of the river in summer and climb the bluff to find arrowheads and buffalo bones. The way the wind is blowing, they'll be digging for this town, next.

Her stomach growls.

Across the street is a convenience store. Ducking her head into her coat collar, Beth Anne leaves her shelter and crosses the street. She passes the self-service gas pump and finds herself facing two small figures in blue jeans and blue jean jackets. The lounging Juneau girls, who, in spite of their flimsy clothing, show the cold only in their glowing red cheeks.

"I've got to go in the store," Beth Anne pleads.

The older girl inspects her with her inquisitive black eyes. "Loan us a dollar."

"I don't have that much," Beth Anne lies.

"How were you going to buy something in the store, then?"

Both girls stand close to Beth Anne. She gets a whiff of unwashed denim and the flesh of young girls. The oldest girl is almost as tall as Beth Anne, and when she stands on tiptoe, she can look down into Beth Anne's eyes. Leaning forward until her nose is an inch from Beth Anne's, she leers. "Hey! Loan us a dollar!"

The younger girl grabs at Beth Anne's shoulder bag. The strap is tangled around Beth Anne's arm, but the girl pulls it as far as she can and riffles through it. She giggles when she finds the coin purse.

"Give me that!" yells the older girl at the sight of a loose paper dollar or two. "I said gimme—" she makes a grab at her sister, who dodges and runs. A quarter spins away in the snow, but the girl keeps running. Her fluting giggle rings out.

"You fucker!" shouts the older girl. She abandons Beth Anne and chases her sister.

Beth Anne watches until the two girls disappear around the corner of the implement dealership. Then she shakes the snow off her coin purse and hunts, scuffing snow with her feet, but the quarter is gone forever, or at least until spring thaw. Beth

Anne begins to shake. She leans against the ice machine and lets the seizure of violent twitches run its course.

Will the imps haunt her for the rest of her life? All winter? Maybe they'll lose interest. When will that be?

And what are you going to do about it?

"I don't know," says Beth Anne. A man in an expensive polyester overcoat just coming out of the convenience store gives her a quick suspicious look and keeps walking.

She leans against the ice machine and listens to the wind. Last summer's canopy of colored flags above the gas pumps has never been taken down, and the wind tears at the little colored triangles and winds them around their ropes. They make a familiar, desolate sound. Beth Anne listens. When she was about twelve, and just before he took his own life, her father had taken her out to her grandmother's old farm north of town for some reason and set beer bottles in a line and shot at them with a twenty-two rifle. The rifle had pop-popped and the wind had whined through the grass with the same insistence.

Poor little girl, said her mother. Poor little fatherless girl. Beth Anne tastes the remembered words, chews them over. Pity. Pity. A word for what she doesn't dare feel, not for herself.

She's broke, and the support check from Pete, if he sends it, isn't due until the first of next month. On feet that feel as though they have frozen solid, she turns and walks slowly back down the street.

The bank clock shows one-fifteen when she stops outside the front entrance of the Beth Anne Shop. She leans into the plate glass to see through the silver and white decorator foliage in the window. Probably Florence called Cindy Lawson to come and take Beth Anne's place while Florence went for a late lunch. Beth Anne takes the chance that it's only Cindy and opens the door.

The plush and brocade hothouse is silent and empty, but the door jingles, and Cindy looks up from reading *Mademoiselle*. Her eyes widen.

Beth Anne walks straight to the cash register and punches it open with stiff purple fingers. She tries to think how much she might need. She doesn't want to run Florence short with the banks closing tomorrow. Slowly she counts out ten twenties and stuffs them in her coat pocket.

Cindy makes a small sound from behind her fingers. Under her mop of professionally frizzed hair she looks like a scared rag doll.

"I just borrowed two hundred. Mom wants me to work after Christmas. I'll pay it back then," says Beth Anne to reassure her.

Halfway to the door she remembers that, since she isn't going back to college, she can work for her mother clear through the January sales. She turns to tell Cindy and catches her in motion.

"I . . . I just," Cindy stammers.

"You can call Florence. I don't care."

As she turns her back she sees Cindy's reflection, superimposed against the snow on the plate glass, with the blue telephone pressed against her reddish hair.

10

The rancher is a grandson of Basque immigrants who came as sheepherders to the shortgrass prairie of northern Montana at the turn of the century, built up a flock of their own, and, by virtue of doing without amenities like coffee and sugar that their neighbors regarded as necessities, managed to save enough to buy up abandoned homesteads during the terrible drought years of the twenties. What they got, they hung on to. The rancher remembers the old people very well, for they lived on into their eighties. Their struggle drained their sap until they shriveled like dried chokecherries, but they kept adding to their land and their sheep, and they passed on to the grandson the means for a comfortable living that they had taught him not to enjoy.

He has sent his own children to the small state college in Versailles, fifty miles from home, but he still lives in the small frame house that was plumbed and wired for electricity in the fifties, and he denies himself and his wife the smallest pleasures. Well, Christmas presents maybe. But the precepts he inherited from the old people are burned into him like a permanent brand. The land comes first. Then the sheep. Then the children. There are no other priorities.

This fall, concerned about the effects of a dry summer and early snow on his overgrazed range, he has decided that it would be no bad move to cull and ship his flocks earlier than he usually does. Yesterday, therefore, after listening to the market reports during these last days of 1972, and with an ear to what he thinks might be a temporary increase in the price of sheep, he has cut out a hundred young replacement ewes and penned them in the small pasture below the shed. The rest of his flocks left this morning at dawn on the trucks for the two-hundred-and-fifty-mile ride down to the livestock auction in Billings.

11

Beth Anne studies the rack at the convenience store and chooses a sack of cake doughnuts drenched in powdered sugar. She pulls the roll of bills out of her pocket and clumsily extracts a twenty. Her fingers are so stiff that she can hardly hang on to it.

The boy at the cash register, a college student in a pearl-snapped western shirt with his name on plastic pinned to his pocket, looks at her curiously. "Say, weren't you talking to them kids a little while ago?"

"Yes," says Beth Anne. She picks up her change and stuffs it, coins and all, into her pocket with the other bills.

"You better be careful. We've caught them girls shoplifting so many times the boss he won't even let them through the door."

"Okay," says Beth Anne, opening her sack of doughnuts on the way to the door. The few pedestrians on East First glance at her as she trudges along munching her doughnuts, but she pays no attention. By the time she reaches the sporting goods store she's polished off half the sack.

Beth Anne walks past the acrylic Christmas trees hung with fishing lures. She mops at her face with her coat sleeve. Underlying the acrid powder smell that stung her nose when she came through the door is the warm greasy odor of new hardware. Very different from the Beth Anne Shop. But rows of overhead fluorescent lights over an expanse of carpet deaden the sound of the storm, and mirrors shine from odd angles. Like the Beth Anne Shop, more is being sold here than merchandise.

The clerk glances around, incurious at first, then with more interest as Beth Anne takes the next to the last doughnut from her sack and stuffs it in her mouth.

"Can I help you?"

"Just looking," Beth Anne says hastily, through the doughnut.

The clerk turns back to the man in the parka.

"So how's coyote hunting?"

The man in the parka has pale, cropped hair and pale blue eyes like marbles in an unlined face. He looks familiar, but Beth Anne wanders all the way along a row of rifles and finds the case of handguns before she recognizes him out of police uniform.

"We got forty-two yesterday. This snow makes 'em stand out."

"Forty-two, I'll be damned."

"Hell, we got it down to an art. We took the right door off the Citabria, and I fly, and Jake he shoots pretty straight. But it's colder'n the devil's pecker up at altitude with the door off the plane."

"Pelts worth much?"

"Hundred, maybe a hundred and twenty at the auctions in Canada. For good pelts. And I got a thousand stretched and stacked in my garage."

The clerk adds in his head. "Jesus."

The big man laughs. "Them coyote pelts, they're the big fashion over in Europe."

Beth Anne looks through the glass at the display of handguns. She had come into the store with vague thoughts of her father's rifle, but now it occurs to her that a handgun would be easier to carry. All she knows about pistols is that they come in different calibers, but she forgets to wonder what a caliber might be, because something about the silent, businesslike row of guns has made her catch her breath.

A blue-burnished gun in a red velvet case draws her eye. She leans over the case, breathing powdered sugar on the glass, to get a better look at the long, archaic barrel and the polished grip that reminds her of old movies with duels and swordplay.

"Did you want to look at one of them black-powder guns?" the clerk calls from the front of the store. "Big hobby now, black powder."

"Just looking." Then she remembers her decision. "I mean, I have to make up my mind."

The clerk shrugs. "Bet that plane of yours is full of fleas," he says.

He and the big man laugh together, stretching out the slow afternoon.

"I suppose it's just a matter of time until you clean the country out of coyotes altogether," remarks the clerk.

"Yeah, and everybody's trying to get a chunk. Last week I even seen a helicopter cruising for coyotes east of Big Sandy. I'd sure like to get over to Browning as soon as this storm passes through. They got coyotes and even wolves on the reservation, and hell, the tribal council wants 'em hunted, they don't care. I'd sneak over there before the boys from Fish and Game ever caught on."

"Would you shoot a wolf?"

"Wouldn't dare shoot a wolf. They got wolves on the endangered species list. They'd have my balls."

Outside the plate glass, the street has grown darker. The headlights of a few early cars shine through blowing snow.

"How's Jake doing?"

"Good."

"Damn shame about his leg. Don't suppose he says much."

The policeman shifts himself against the counter from one buttock to the other. "Him and me, we've thinned them coyotes down, all right. But you remember how the state hunters spread 1080 in this country back in the forties? My dad thought he'd never see another coyote. But they came back."

"Well, take care, Mike."

Beth Anne turns back to the pistols. She longs to hold the lovely archaic gun in her hands and stroke the balanced line of the barrel. For the first time she notices that a tiny wild thing is etched on the grip. An antelope or deer. She sees the price tag. Nearly three hundred dollars.

Assorted cheaper handguns, conventional revolvers, are arranged on glass shelves. Beth Anne reads the price tags. Two hundred dollars. One hundred dollars.

The clerk comes down the counter, looking at his wrist-watch. "What you got in mind?"

Beth Anne puts her hand in her coat pocket and feels for her roll of bills. "I want to buy a gun."

"Handgun?"

He waits, but she doesn't know what to say.

"Well, what are you going to use it for?"

The question catches her off guard. She feels blood rise in her face. She doesn't exactly intend to shoot the Juneau girls, and yet here she is.

"Self-defense?" suggests the clerk. "A lot of women are scared to be alone at night."

Behind the thick lenses of his glasses, his eyes are a blur, as if she's not quite in focus for him.

"Self-defense, yes. That's what I want it for."

"Twenty-two's good for that." He dives behind the counter and comes up with a small square box. "Here's a nice little piece. Only cost you eighty-nine ninety-eight."

He opens the box with his soft fingers and shows her the small revolver. It's got a short black barrel, a stainless steel cylinder, and a white plastic grip scored to look like ivory. It looks real.

"See, this is the pin, and you pull it out here." He shows her how to load the cylinder and cock the hammer. "It'll be fairly accurate up to a hundred feet or so. After that, not so precise. But for what you want . . ."

Beth Anne's hands close around the ugly little grip. The gun is much heavier than it looks, but she knows it will fit easily into her shoulder bag.

"You know how to sight it?"

He shows her how to stretch the gun at arm's length. How to aim. She sees a row of goose decoys fade out of focus on the other side of the store as the black metal sights take shape and sharpen.

"And you'll need a box of shells. You want long rifle or short?"

"Ah . . ."

"Long, most likely."

He selects a tiny cardboard carton from a shelf and lays it on the counter. Beth Anne picks up the little box as he goes to ring up the sale and finds it as unexpectedly heavy as the revolver.

"Now I gotta ask you some questions," says the clerk, coming back with her change. "State of Montana law. Everybody that buys a handgun has to answer all these questions by saying no."

Beth Anne repeats the words to herself, trying to think what they mean.

"No big deal," he explains, "but I can't sell you the gun unless you answer no to all these questions. You ever been committed to a mental institution?"

Beth Anne opens her mouth and shuts it in bewilderment, and the young man glances up from his list of questions. "Just answer no! You haven't been, have you?"

"No!"

"All right, then. Have you ever been dishonorably discharged from the armed services?"

"No."

"Renounced your citizenship? Fugitive from justice?"

"No."

He clears his throat, losing his place on the list. "Are you an alien illegally in the United States?"

"What?"

"You didn't sneak in from Mexico or anything, did you? You belong here, don't you?"

"I guess so," she whispers.

"Then say no!"

"No!"

"Are you under indictment from any court for a crime that could be punishable by a sentence that would exceed one year?"

"No," says Beth Anne. Her ears are ringing.

"Have you ever been convicted by any court of a crime that could be punishable by a sentence that would exceed one year?"

He glances up and explains, "That means it don't matter whether you really got the sentence. It means could you have got the sentence."

"Oh," says Beth Anne. "No," she adds hastily.

"Okay, that's all there is to it," he says with relief. He hands her the package of gun and shells, neatly wrapped together in strong white paper.

Beth Anne makes room for the package in her shoulder bag. The unusual weight drags at her arm as she makes for the door. She wonders if the lovely burnished pistol in the velvet dueling case would have been less burdensome. She looks back once, but the clerk has busied himself with the cash register tallies, and she's pretty sure he's already forgotten her.

12

After supper the rancher walks down as far as the pasture fence and smokes a cigarette. It's already too dark to see the ewes clearly, and too cold to be comfortable standing around out of doors, but he listens to the sounds of the flock settling down for the night. Pale shapes. Stamps and creaks and rumbles of full bellies, bleats and answering baas. The warm smell of sheep, ragged wool, and droppings. Not a ewe in the pasture that he hasn't raised, fed, sheared, and doctored when necessary. Not a ewe that, like any good sheepman, he couldn't pick out as his own. Not that he feels a single qualm about the eventual fate of his flocks as fat lambs and slaughter ewes, and not that he would ever say it out loud, or even admit it to himself, but he's fond of his sheep. He likes being near the young ewes, stinking wool and all.

And so he loiters out there for a good fifteen minutes, listening to the sheep bedding down and watching the moon rise over the low bluff behind his sheds and corrals. The yard light he's recently had installed over the house burns steadily. The early evening is already getting colder, the next Canadian storm front is on its way. He drops his cigarette butt on the bare ground and scuffs out the glowing end with the toe of his boot. More snow is coming. He knows his decision to ship the rest of his sheep had been a good one.

Hell no, he'll say later. Never crossed my mind. Never thought a goddamn thing about it. I knew I had them young ewes behind a good tight sheep fence. I went back to the house and went to bed. Hell, them ewes wasn't for chrissake but fifty yards from my bedroom window.

13

Darkness has fallen and suddenly First Street is alive with early celebrants who hoot and jostle their way between the Jubilee and the Palace, the Eagles and the Vets Club and the Golden Spike and the Glacier Bar and the Hackamore. Beth Anne stumps along through the patches of red and green lights with the rest of the crowd. She doesn't look at the heavily bundled revelers who bump into her from time to time, she's not concerned with them. In spite of the lopsided weight of the package in her purse, she's barely aware, even, of the snowpacked sidewalk. Her feet are hurting her badly. Maybe she's frostbitten them. She's heard that frostbite kills feeling.

She tells herself she might as well stop at the Jubilee and get warm before she commences the long uphill climb home. And after the five o'clock crowd on First Street, the Jubilee seems almost quiet. Several tables are vacant, and Beth Anne chooses a secluded one, against the wall.

"A brandy ditch," she says boldly when the barmaid, not the aloof golden-haired barmaid of last night, but a friendlier girl in a ruffled red blouse and a short black skirt comes to take her order. She looks around, loosening her coat. It's a different crowd from last night, an earlier crowd. Older men, mostly, killing time with a drink before they have to go home and wrap presents. The television above the bar is running some kind of special newscast with its volume turned down. Beth Anne watches a scene of pilgrims in Jerusalem as it changes without transition into a crowd scene outside the Vatican.

Her drink arrives, golden and full of ice. Beth Anne digs one of her twenties from her coat pocket and watches the barmaid count out a stack of crumpled singles. She takes a deep swallow, anxious to get past the first bad taste. Her feet are dead weights, and she bends down to look, but it's too dark under the table to see them. She knows she should have been wearing snowboots instead of the pumps she dug out of the closet this morning to wear to work in the Beth Anne Shop.

The TV changes from a frame of frantic Christmas shoppers to a shot of soldiers in combat gear walking along a road through strange yellow fields, and then to a close-up of a commentator with a mustache in the middle of his earnest face. Beth Anne shifts in her chair so she can't see him. After all, he isn't real. He's a flash on the screen. She doesn't have to take him seriously.

She sips her brandy. That's always been her trouble, taking things too seriously. Raymond took everything seriously. The first time she ever saw him, he was sitting upright in his chair in the current events class with his eyes bright with gloom. Trying to please him, Beth Anne learned statistics about suicide rates and alcoholism on reservations as she once had memorized high school football scores.

The barmaid sets another full golden glass in front of her. Beth Anne can't remember ordering another drink, but she's in no hurry to walk home. She lets the barmaid sort out a dollar bill from her stack and take away the empty glass. Except for her feet, she feels fine.

"Jake! Hey, shotgun man! How's the hunting?"

"Forty-two yesterday."

"No shit."

"At least you guys can get out in the plane now and then. Christ! That must be an experience. Especially when there's snow."

"They stand out against the snow, all right."

"The big danger is getting tangled up in the power lines."

Beth Anne imagines the pair of wild dogs, furred, racing across the snowy fields, trying to reach the shelter of a coulee ahead of the pursuing shadow. The plane banks sharply, fifty feet above the power lines, and the shotgunner takes aim.

She jerks awake. The lights in the bar seem brighter now, or maybe it's her imagination. Another golden drink, brimful, sits before her. Brandy slops over the glass when she reaches for it. She can't remember whether it's her third or fourth drink, or how long her feet have been throbbing.

"My dad knew a fellow, years ago, that hunted coyotes with a pair of rat terriers. A male and a female. He'd send the terriers down a coyote den to bring the pups out. He needed the scalps for the bounty, of course. Well, the old male dog would go down into a den and kill the pups and fetch them out one at a time, dead. But the female would carry the pups out alive and start to lick them. Animals sure can be human."

"You call that human?" somebody snickered.

"Hell, a coyote'll kill her own pups if she thinks some-body's fouled her den."

Somebody is standing over her. "Beth Anne?"

"She's been pouring them right down," agrees somebody.

Beth Anne squints and sees a balding head and sharp dark eyes under heavy eyebrows. He's pulling at her elbow, angry for some reason.

"Hell, Bud, let her alone."

"I'm just going to see she gets home. Least I can do for Pete."

"Bud," says the golden-haired barmaid, who somewhere in the past hour or two has replaced the friendly girl. "Bud, you're drunk, too."

Beth Anne tries to explain that her feet hurt, but he tugs so insistently that at last she makes the attempt to stand.

"Leave her alone, Bud."

More shadows hover over her. A chair leg thumps down.

"What the hell she did to Pete is what I'd like to know. Jesuschrist, best goddamn natural athlete I ever saw, and she—"

"Go home yourself, Bud."

"—all the natural ability in the world. The first time he turned out for practice we knew we had a team. And now look at us. We'll all be socialists in ten years. Julie doesn't know what the fuck it's all about."

Beth Anne opens her eyes. She sees the man in the black cowboy hat. Jake, the shotgun man. He's not bad-looking, maybe some Indian in him, it shows in his straight black hair and the thick set of his shoulders. His stiffened leg evokes some past violence done to him, and yet he's steady-voiced and steady-handed, as though he's willing to take a chance on worse things happening to him.

"You don't want to stay here all night, do you?"

At his patient prodding she stuffs her brandy-soaked bills into her coat pocket and hobbles around the table and the over-turned chair and past the flashing TV over the bar. She wants to explain that she isn't drunk, it's just that her feet burn. But the door opens, and the first breath she draws is so icy that she wonders if her lungs have been blasted dry.

The shotgun man is boosting her into a pickup truck and slamming the door on her. She hears his boots crunching on the snow as he limps around to the driver's side. The cab of the truck is cold and claustrophobic, and it smells acrid, it smells of blood and something else, something wild. She has never felt a cold so deep. The lighted thermometer on the bank across the street reads minus thirty-two degrees.

The shotgun man grinds the unwilling motor into life and steers slowly past the Jubilee. Red and green lights flicker through the cab and disappear when he turns off the downtown streets. Beth Anne recognizes the new building that Bud Burchette's real estate office shares with an insurance company and a law firm. There have been so many forced entries this winter that more and more businessmen have been taking the glass out of their windows and filling them with bricks and mortar. The fortified windows give the town a look of siege under the reflection of Christmas lights and the solid cloud of exhaust that hangs suspended in the frozen night.

The shotgun man's truck makes short work of Beth Anne's long walk, taking the hill easily with its snow tires crunching and its headlights sweeping over her landlady's snow-shrouded yard and Beth Anne's own car buried in snow by the curb.

The shotgun man stops, lets his motor idle.

"I remember you from high school, Beth," he says. "We had the same English class when I transferred up here, senior year."

She nods.

"Dunno what you're looking for in the Jubilee," he says.

Beth Anne fights hard to stay awake, because she still has to climb the treacherous flight of steps and unlock her apartment door. But the cab of the truck is warm now. She lets her eyelids sink, drags them open. Wonders what happened to lame the shotgun man. Wonders if she's going to be lame. Remembers. No pity for herself, no pity.

"—you're missing them kids, right? But Pete's bringing them back tomorrow. You don't want to be hanging around downtown getting in trouble when they come home."

Her head has never felt so heavy. When she lets it sink into the back of the seat, she feels her body spread and grow heavier. Mountains and gullies and plains under a deepening blanket of sleep. The furred creatures race across her for the shelter of her crevices. She rouses herself and gropes for her shoulder bag.

The shotgun man is telling her something. He's saying something important. Says he knows how she feels, says he had a kid once. People say good things about him, but he knows he did the wrong thing, knows he sure as hell did. She nods and steps out carefully into a snowbank up to her knees.

When she looks around, the shotgun man's truck is pulling away with its tires complaining on the snowpack. Through the rear window she catches a last glimpse just of the outline of his head in the nimbus from the dash.

A light cracks the shade in a downstairs window. Her landlady, looking to see whose truck has been sitting so long in front of her house with its engine running.

Bile has frozen on her chin, but the cold air helps to clear her head. On her fiery feet she wades through fresh snow and climbs the flight of steps, clinging to the banister to keep from slipping on the ice that has thickened treacherously under the snow. She ducks her head under the chattering branches of the cottonwood tree and opens the door on silence and stale dark air.

As she turns on the light, her pupils contract and then clear. She sees the scarred stove and sink, the dirty table and garbage pail, all undisturbed since morning. Taped to the refrigerator door is the last drawing Emily brought home from school, a Christmas tree in quivering green and red wax like a wound on the blank regulation paper. The stick figures of a family lurk behind the tree. A mother with a baby in her arms, a shadowy father with a small stick boy held in either hand. The signature is straight and neat for a second grader. Emily Anne Vanago, age 7, Hawthorne School.

Emily, why can't you color inside the lines? Why do you bear down so hard? Here, honey, let grandma show you how.

I like to bear down hard. Let me color like I want to.

Beth Anne tears off her girdle, letting her panty hose twist around the heavy elastic, and throws the whole tangle into a corner. She sits down on the side of the bed and inspects her feet. In spite of the throb, they look white and dead. She can't think of a way to make them stop hurting, so at last she gives up and limps out to the kitchen. Everything's just as she left it. An empty glass with a crusty white pool in its bottom is glued to the table by a dried river of tomato juice. John must have waked up, found himself alone, and gone away without leaving a trace of himself.

Beth Anne shoves away plates and glasses to clear a space on the table. She picks loose the knotted string and tears the paper off the revolver and the box of cartridges. The gun looks shiny and efficient against the litter on the table. Beth Anne shakes several of the little bullets out of their box. They look smug as seeds, too small to shatter one bottle after another into deep August grass, or even glance and whine against a pebble.

Beth Anne pulls out the pin as the clerk had taught her. Her heart begins to thump as she picks up the little bullets, one by one, and slides them into the chambers of the cylinder. Puzzled at the way her body is reacting, she snaps back the cylinder and shakily replaces the pin. Her heartbeat is so insistent that she looks down and sees its soft pulse, pulse, pulse under her sweater.

Her fingers find the little button that's the safety. She pushes it free. If she pulled the trigger now, the gun would fire. Carefully she returns it to the safety position. Then off. On. Off. On. Or is it off? Is she mixed up? Is she absolutely certain the gun wouldn't fire? Yes. No. Not absolutely. Heart pounding crazily, Beth Anne raises the gun in both hands and aims down the sights at the refrigerator and squeezes the trigger. Nothing happens. Her heart lurches. She gasps and lowers the gun to give in to the tide of relief.

When she feels able, Beth Anne leans on the table and hoists herself out of the chair. The discarded wrapping paper drifts to the floor as she hobbles into the bedroom with the revolver. She lays it down on the bed by the wall and sinks into the welcoming sag on the side of the bed that had been Pete's.

14

Coyotes will eat anything from carrion to grasshoppers, mice, gophers, rabbits, fawns, poultry, house cats, lambs, calves, even adult animals that are old enough or sick enough to be run down and dragged down. During the drought years of the twenties, when the ranchers on the northern plains were trying to earn a few cash dollars by raising flocks of turkeys on their blighted acres, coyotes were their scourge. Sheep ranchers and cattle ranchers had always despised coyotes, and now the turkey farmers carried rifles in saddle scabbards or on racks in pickup trucks to snatch down and shoot at coyotes on sight. They set traps for coyotes, they hunted them with greyhounds, and they laid out poisoned bait, but still the coyotes survived.

For years the government paid a bounty on coyote scalps, and, finally, in the forties, sponsored the massive distribution of the poison 1080 which, concealed in the carcasses of cattle or deer, not only wiped out the coyotes, but crows, owls, magpies—all the predators of rodents. Jackrabbits and gophers and mice proliferated. And the coyotes, no longer a scourge but a symbol of the vanishing West, withdrew from their old haunts in draws and coulees and sang no more sad songs from the hills at night.

If somebody had told me ten years ago that I'd be taking a kid of mine to a wildlife exhibit to see a coyote, I'd have laughed at the dumb son of a bitch, the rancher remembers saying in 1955.

Then one evening in the early sixties, he sat up straight in his chair.

Would have sworn I heard a coyote.

I thought so too, said his wife. They both listened. There it is again, she said.

I'll be goddamned. After all these years. Sounds kinda . . . good, was what he almost said, but he stopped himself in time. Sounds kinda familiar, he said instead.

15

At three thousand feet the short-lived afternoon sun shines very bright, burning across the cowling of the Citabria and dazzling in red and blue flashes on the windshield. Above the plane the shreds and tatters of ragged overcast race west and expose patches of brilliant blue sky at thirty thousand feet. Below, reflecting the shadow of the plane like a dancing cross, the deep white and unbroken blue snow stretches like a polar field to the horizon where the snowbound Milk River valley opens east between wavering double lines of the primordial riverbed. A giant flow of water once cut between those dim blue bluffs in a time before human remembering. This afternoon, from five hundred feet aloft, the valley blazes back with sheer white and blue and gray, but somewhere under the ice and snow that buries all landmarks, the river stays alive in its shrunken channel. Further east, the dark gray tops of the leafless cottonwoods follow the river like a line of miniature brushwork that leads to an unrevealed dimension and fades to invisibility through the unstable atmosphere.

"It's blowing like a bitch down there," comes Mike's voice through the headset.

Jake, riding shotgun in the rear seat, nods. Without the right door his face is numb and his bad leg an icicle of pain, but the sun shines as brightly as though it will never again be obliterated by a storm. And yet Mike, at the controls in the front seat, is pointing to the eastern horizon where the dark storm cell lies. From their altitude it takes on a distinct shape and motion, like a swarm blotting out light.

Mike is pointing again. Jake catches the flicker of life across the white, empty prairie, makes out the minute dark fleeing shape. The snowfields loom up as Mike dives and banks in pursuit. From fifty feet off the ground Jake sees, out of the corner of his eye, ice on the power lines and snow blowing like smoke across the highway as Mike cuts the coyote off from the safety of a coulee. When he feels Mike's weight shift, he aims the shotgun. He looks into the furious golden eyes for just an instant as he hears the shotgun blast.

The power lines are coming up fast. He feels and hears Mike feed full throttle as they swoop over the lines. Mike banks again. The coyote, miniaturized by distance, thrashes in the red-stained snow.

"You got him," rasps Mike through the headset. "But do you see anywhere to set down?"

Jake points to the next stubble field, where the snow has blown thin, and Mike circles around to head east and into the wind. The field rises under them as he wrestles the plane, silent with its engine dead, crabwise against the gusts of wind on the ground. The blue cross of the Citabria's shadow rises to merge with them, and then the tail wheel is tearing through the snow while Mike holds off the nose and brakes within ten feet of the snow fence along Highway 2.

They're within fifty feet of the dead coyote.

"You mean I got to walk clear over there?" Mike complains. "Hell, I could have landed on that knoll."

"Like hell you could have."

Jake's face is so numb that he feels only the staccato of frozen snow granules when they rattle into his eyes. He eases his bad leg out of the rear seat and beats his hands against his thighs. From the ground the sun seems much farther away than it does from the air.

"Still gives you misery?" asks Mike.

"My leg?"

"Ain't nothing else that ought to be giving you misery."

The snow has drifted deeply into the coulee between them and the coyote. Mike breaks trail through a hip-deep crust and holds the shotgun while Jake crawls through the barbed wire fence. Panting clouds of white, they come upon the coyote.

It lies still by now, its eyes glazed, the snow honeycombed with its blood. A big female, its prime fur disguising the paucity of its belly and thighs. The shotgun blast had caught it in the shoulder, breaking the foreleg. Mike prods it with the toe of his boot, making sure it's dead, and unfolds his plastic garbage bag.

Working as fast as they can with stiff hands, they maneuver the corpse into the plastic bag and seal it. Jake hefts his end of the load and looks back at the plane, a red toy in the expanse of white and glittering blue. The ground is unsubstantial, and the only sound is their own breathing. The storm is moving in fast, and already the snowfields are reduced by the fading light to a sullen waste. The sky seems shrunken.

"Bet this bastard don't weigh fifty pounds," says Mike. "Been a bad year for coyotes, too."

They make their way out into the stubble where the going is easier. Back at the plane they sling their burden into the rear compartment with the other frozen carcasses and buckle themselves in.

Mike guns the throttle and taxis around in a tight circle to the far end of the stubble field. The wind is stiff now, and the Citabria jounces over snow and frozen sod.

"How come we're starting clear back here?" says Jake into his headset. "How much of a run do you need?"

"I'm no shotgun pilot like some folks. I'm careful."

"Fuck you."

Mike turns the Citabria into the wind and gives it full throttle. The stubble blurs as the plane bounces and gains speed. The snow fence rushes toward them. At the last minute Jake feels the airlift. Freed, the plane clears the snow fence and soars over the drifts and shallows. The earth falls away. Mike banks and turns toward the lights of Versailles that are beginning to wink from the river valley.

"Wonder how bad the runway drifted since this morning."

"Maybe they plowed it."

"Don't look like it."

The sky has turned dark blue. The airport beacon flashes against the stained clouds, and the runway lights materialize like a row of pinpricks through a dark blanket. Mike cuts throttle, and the plane settles silently down. Snow drags at the wheels.

16

Beth Anne fights her way out of a dream in which she was flying down a tunnel and emerged only to become enmeshed in a web of power lines. She struggles and gets the telephone off the hook on the ninth or tenth ring.

"Hello?" she says thickly.

"Beth Anne!" Her mother's voice is flooded with relief. "I've been trying all night to reach you."

Beth Anne's mouth tastes poisonous. The bed revolves slowly around the telephone. But when she touches the floor with her feet, the instant agony stops the bed.

"I let the phone ring and ring, but you didn't answer— Bethie, you're all right, aren't you?"

Beth Anne slides back down into the warm tangle of blankets, shutting her eyes. "I've been asleep," she whispers.

"Ever since Florence called, I've been worried sick, and I couldn't imagine where you might have gone on Christmas Eve—"

Beth Anne tries to lick her lips, but her tongue is too woolly. "Mom, I was going to work for you over vacation, the money was just an advance—"

"Florence said she didn't want to worry me, but she didn't know what else to do. She said she'd ask you a direct question and you'd stare as if you'd never seen her before."

A pause. Then her mother's anxious words spill out of the phone. "First she thought you'd been drinking, but she couldn't *smell* anything, and then it crossed her mind—and Julie Burchette had heard—honey, you haven't been *taking* anything?"

She's still thinking about the money. "Taking what?"

"Just your Valium. You've been taking that, haven't you?"

Beth Anne can't remember if she has or not. "Yes."

Her mother's breath lets out in sibilant relief. "Oh, honey, over the vacation we'll spend some time together. We'll have lunch."

"I'm okay," Beth Anne whispers into the telephone with her eyes shut, but her mother's voice, fragile as a young girl's, patters on her ear.

"Honey, it hasn't been so easy for me, either, not lately, and I know you don't want to hear about it. But I'll call you tomorrow, all right?"

Beth Anne lies on her back with her eyes shut, holding the phone to her ear. Suddenly she doesn't want to hang up.

"All right? Beth Anne?"

"Sure," Beth Anne whispers into the receiver. "Bye," she whispers, and listens until she hears the faint, faraway click.

She doesn't replace the receiver until she hears the dial tone resume. Then she sits up and tries her feet on the floor again. Her feet feel hot and puffy, and she has to grit her teeth to stand on them, and then she feels her soles deflate under her as if she had stepped on two fresh loaves of bakery bread. She turns on the bedroom light. Staring at her from the mirror above the row of photographs on the dresser is a woman with a swollen white face and eyes like burnt holes under a tangle of dirty hair.

Maybe she should call the doctor about her feet. But after a step or two the pain is not quite so anguishing. She limps into the bathroom and sits on the toilet without bothering to close the door. Emptying her bladder is a pleasure. She leans on her knees with the toilet seat warming under her and wonders what she should do about her feet.

Beth Anne freezes in the act of wiping. She strains her ears. Sometimes the cottonwood twigs make eerie scratching sounds against the wooden steps outside, especially in the wind. The children were afraid of the sounds, or pretended to be, when they first moved into the apartment. Every time the wind blew they wanted to get in bed with her or move back to their old house. But there's no wind tonight. She's certain it wasn't twigs she heard. She tries to remember if she had locked the door behind her. Sometimes the old latch doesn't come across unless she stops and punches it.

Somebody turns the knob. Beth Anne leaps off the toilet. Her knees almost buckle under her from the outrage of her feet, but she pulls down her skirt and takes a silent, excruciating giant step into the bedroom. She switches off the bedroom light just as a light comes on in the kitchen.

John. He forgot his wallet, or something, and she hadn't noticed, but now he's coming back for it. But she doesn't care, because she's had time to crawl over the foot of the bed and burrow under the blankets until her fingers close around the smooth, cool butt of the revolver. She holds the gun behind her and faces the door. John's in for a surprise.

Something crashes in the kitchen. Broken glass tinkles in the sink. Somebody giggles, and suddenly Beth Anne knows for certain who's out there. Holding the revolver behind her, she steals out of the bedroom and into the hall in spite of the pain that screams all the way to her knees.

"Hey! Fatso! How come you turned your light off?"

She looks past an overturned chair into two pairs of dark almond eyes.

"Hey, Fatso!"

The older girl had stopped whatever she was doing at the sight of Beth Anne. Her sister, who had been rifling through Beth Anne's shoulder bag, stares over her shoulder and draws the bag up against herself.

"This all you got?" she demands, regaining her poise.

The rest of Beth Anne's paper money, of course, is still in her coat pocket. She says nothing, but she can hardly keep from laughing as she looks at the two lovely peach faces screwed up impudently at her and thinks how surprised the girls are going to be. She feels her stomach start to shake with laughter.

"You'd better put my purse down," she warns, to be fair.

Both faces turn defiant. "You can't tell us what to do."

"You fat fucker," says the older girl, starting toward Beth Anne, just as Beth Anne, remembering to release the safety, raises the revolver from behind her back.

In the abrupt silence, the refrigerator turns on and hums.

"That's real!" says the older girl. Her voice sounds so surprised and natural with the arrogance drained out that Beth Anne again has to fight back laughter.

The girl assesses how far away her sister is. Then she turns on Beth Anne and bares her teeth like a kitten. Beth Anne has to admire her nerve. Pete, she thinks, would have started out by trying to convince her that girls couldn't shoot guns, and then, when he saw that she wouldn't back down, he would have collapsed. But the Juneau girls hold their ground and snarl at her. And it might just be TV that has taught them the scenario, but Beth Anne still thinks that if she could start all over again as somebody else, she wouldn't mind doing it as one of the Juneau girls. Them kids, their grandfather always called them. I'll whale them kids when they get home.

Beth Anne levels the gun in both hands at shoulder height. The younger girl lets out a small mew and shrinks closer to her sister. It's the first sign of fear Beth Anne has seen in her. And for a split second Beth Anne wavers. She can't aim at both girls at once, so she sights down the barrel on the older girl's whitened eye. Nothing happens when she squeezes the trigger, so she yanks on it as hard as she can.

The explosion from the gun exceeds any climax she could have dreamed of. Her ears reverberate as smoke and the smell settle down over the dirty dishes and the garbage on the kitchen table and the overturned chairs. She's got no idea what she hit, but she didn't hit either of the girls. They're backed up against the sink, hanging on to each other and looking so astonished that Beth Anne has to laugh out loud.

The younger girl begins to cry with her mouth square, the way Emily or the baby would have cried. And before it occurs to Beth Anne that she could take another shot at them, they're both grappling with the kitchen doorknob. It takes them several tries to turn it. Each pushing to get through the door ahead of the other, they bolt for the landing. Beth Anne hears them whimpering and crashing and sliding their way down the icy steps. There's a last crash at the bottom, and Beth Anne hobbles to the door in time to see the girls trying to run through the snowdrift that has buried the yard. In the glow of the streetlight, they're leaving a trail that looks as though a pair of walruses are making a frantic escape.

Beth Anne drops down in the one chair still on its legs and laughs. She wraps her arms around her sides and rocks back and forth and laughs. Every time she remembers how the girls bumped and shouldered each other through the door, she laughs harder.

When she stops laughing, she hobbles around the kitchen to see where her shot went. After several minutes of searching she finds the hole in the kitchen windowpane, a foot higher than the girls' heads. It's smaller than her finger and perfectly round.

The phone rings.

"Hello?" she says, cautiously.

"Mrs. Vanago?" It's her landlady, all right.

"Yes?" Beth Anne tries to sound sleepy. She yawns into the receiver.

"You were asleep?"

She tries another yawn. "What time is it?"

"Almost seven. I was just pouring my tea, and . . ." A pause. "You didn't hear anything?"

"Hear what?"

"Well, it sounded like some kind of explosion to me. I couldn't tell exactly where it came from. But then there was a crash on the steps. I thought you'd fell down or something."

"No."

Beth Anne says nothing more, and finally her landlady says, "Well, if nothing's wrong up there—" and hangs up.

Beth Anne yawns in earnest. She limps around the kitchen to shut the door, making sure it's locked this time, and to right the chairs. It's only seven o'clock. She might as well go back to bed. She turns off the lights and curls up in the familiar sag. Just before she falls asleep she thinks how puzzled her landlady is going to be when daylight breaks and she sees the trail through the snowdrift across her front yard, and she has to laugh all over again.

17

As the snow begins to fall, lightly at first, the first few white flakes drifting in the dark, then more and more hard flakes driving straight into the windshield, the young woman turns down the brights on her headlights and bears harder on the accelerator. She had hoped to reach Versailles before the predicted storm; she'd thought she had a few more hours. She leans forward over the wheel, trying to watch the highway and watch for deer or cattle on both verges at the same time. Miles from nowhere, no towns, not even a ranch light, and snow accumulating on the asphalt until she can feel her tires glide and spin under her in a direction she's still in control of but senses she soon might not be. What a world. Abstract, ominous. Snow blots the distinction between night sky and night sagebrush. She tries to look through, not at, the snow that rushes toward the windshield and swirls off. She tries to keep her mind on her driving. It would be so easy to allow herself to be hypnotized by the rushing snow, so easy to slide away into the oblivion of landscape.

She tells herself that this adventure into the northern prairie is still an adventure, that it's still the right choice, that she's not going to be sorry she's driving to fill the sudden opening in the middle of the academic year at the little state college in Versailles at a time when few college teaching jobs exist for young women. She knows she'll stay in the job only for a few years, that she won't have to live forever on this barren rim of the world.

She remembers the arching sky from earlier in the day, and how she watched the transparent air change color as the cold front crept down from the north, and how the broken hills and gullies opened themselves, stark and bare, until the storm blew in front of the moon. Even the storm blows with a certain fierce beauty. She's lost her sense of forward motion, she's suspended out here as though in one of those glass balls of snow that, shaken, fills with spinning flakes that continue and continue and continue.

A thing as dark and shapeless as a shadow streaks in front of her headlights, and she hits the brakes.

18

Beth Anne opens her eyes on the ancient water stains on the ceiling and listens to somebody pounding on the kitchen door.

The bright light of fresh snowfall spills over the bare floor, making transparencies of her tie-dyed curtains.

Finally she swings her feet over the side of the bed and pries her eyelids apart. She notices that her toes and insteps have turned the yellowish green of old bruises, and when she stands up, her feet squish under her.

Snow crystals sparkle across the buried yard and dance through the coated twigs, hurting her eyes when she leans across the sink to see out. Parked in the street beside her own snowbound dead heap is a dark red car, low-slung and chromed and caked with dirty ice and snow around the fenders. Her heart takes wing.

What should she do. Comb her hair? Show some pride, begs her mother. But it's already too late.

"Hey! You passed out in there, or what?"

Beth Anne barks a toe on a chair leg as she hastens to the door. The toe screams, halfway up her shin, but she fumbles back the lock. On the landing waits Pete, his breath vaporizing around his head like a halo. But the freezing air that forces Beth Anne a step back into the kitchen is no colder than his eyes.

"Sorry to get you out of bed! After all, it's only noon!"

She thinks he looks like an angry angel with his reddened cheeks and his fair hair just brushing the collar of his blue ski jacket. Bud Burchette might look like a balding insurance man who's been out of school for years, but Pete still looks like a star.

"I didn't know you were going to get here today," she says at last.

"The kids are too big a claim on your time? You're too busy?"

The cold has set her feet on fire, she can't keep standing in the open door. Pete follows her into the kitchen.

"What stinks in here?" he asks in such an awed voice that for a moment Beth Anne thinks he really wants to know and starts to explain that she thinks something has gone bad in the refrigerator. But Pete is staring at his polished loafers. He's stepped on a potato chip. Beth Anne sees him look at the sticky lake where tomato juice dripped off the table, then at the counter where a plastic container of chip dip has gone green and watery.

"It's a goddamn pigpen in here."

"New Year's," Beth Anne remembers. "That's when you said you were bringing them back."

"Figured you had another week to lay around in bed, did you?"

"I just—"

"Or maybe I interrupted something? Maybe you've got some son of a bitch back there right now?"

"Pete, no, I . . ."

But he's stamping into the bedroom to see for himself. Beth Anne sits heavily and waits for him to discover the emptiness of the apartment. She wonders if she should make a cup of tea. She thinks she has some teabags left. Maybe Pete will drink a cup of tea with her.

The first time he hadn't come home all night she had stayed awake with a pillow pulled over her head to keep from listening for the sound of his car in the driveway, fantasizing him in a car wreck or being beaten up by toughs from the reservation but knowing nothing was wrong except that he'd found something he liked better to do than stay home. Hoping it wasn't the poker game in the back of the Glacier Bar, hoping it was only the poker game.

Honey what am I doing wrong, if you'd just tell me what I'm doing wrong.

Nothing's wrong! Just leave me alone, can't you. Quit whining like I did something to you.

But honey I love you and I get so scared.

Iloveyoutoo but damnit, lemme alone!

The revolver. What if he were to come across it in the bed-covers. How is she going to explain the revolver? But Pete has already searched the bedrooms and the slant-roofed living room and come back to the kitchen, deflated.

"I might as well tell you," he says, "that your mother called me last night."

Beth Anne knows there's a trap in this news. She waits for it to snap.

"She wanted me to come and see you. Give you another chance. Like shit, I told her. Think I'm gonna walk back into a mess like that?"

"No," says Beth Anne and then sees from his face that she has botched her assigned line.

"But I promised her I'd look in on you. Was going to do it anyway, after what Bud said."

Bud Burchette. Last night, last something. She's losing track.

"Bud also told me what kind of trash you've been dragging home with you."

From down in the street a horn blasts long and impatiently.

"You have the kids in the car?"

"Karen's with them. Shit. I told her I'd be right back."

"Who's Karen?"

"My fox."

Beth Anne has never actually heard anyone call a girl a fox. But she can't answer, because her eyes have fallen on the little box of twenty-two shells half under a hamburger wrapper on the table. How could Pete not have noticed it?

"I told your mother it wouldn't be out of my way to look in on you, because Karen and I would be driving up to Versailles this morning to bring the kids home and visit Bud and Julie. But I told her I wasn't staying to watch you sleep your way through every bar on First Street."

She wants to explain that she has slept with only one man from one bar. Raymond she met on campus, he doesn't count as a man from a bar.

"And another thing. I hear about you entertaining your boyfriends in front of those kids, I'll get them taken away from you."

Pete's fists are doubled in knots in rigid line with the seams of his expensive blue jeans. His eyes are livid and blue. It dawns on Beth Anne that he's screaming at her because he wants her to give him something he needs. If she doesn't give it, he's going to work up enough rage to knock her down. She feels dizzy. Beside such a bellow of need, her own voice seems very modest in its *please love me*.

The horn blares again, and Pete stamps over to the window. "I told her I'd be a few minutes. You'd think she'd—"

He glances at Beth Anne and changes what he had been going to say. "Karen's a graduate student at the university. She's producing a documentary film about me."

Beth Anne realizes that he expects her to say something. "Like, one of those on wildlife?"

Pete stares at her. "You don't even know what I'm talking about, do you?"

"No."

"It's going to be about me as a young man in the modern West," he explains. "The effect of open spaces on a man, that kind of thing." He hesitates, doubt clouding his eyes. "If you think you can pull yourself together and clean up this dump before somebody gets sick, I'll go and bring in the kids. But if Karen and I weren't going out with Bud and Julie tonight, I'd keep them with me."

"Okay."

He looks at her, starts to ask a question, changes his mind. A puff of arctic air dances into the kitchen and diffuses as he opens the door and closes it behind him. Beth Anne goes to the window and stands on tiptoe, hoping to catch a glimpse of Karen, but all she can see is the vinyl roof of Pete's car and Pete himself digging children and parcels out of the back seat. Presently she hears them struggling up the steps. Pete staggers in with the baby in her padded snowsuit under one arm and her diaper bag under the other. He looks back over his shoulder.

"The rest of you get in here, god damn it!"

"Jeremy's eating snow."

"I don't give a shit what he eats. Emmy, why can't you help him up those stairs?"

Pete throws a dish towel and a plastic bowl off a chair to make a place to set the baby down. Then he reaches out the door and hauls in the little boys, one after the other. Jeremy's coat and snow pants are so bulky that he can hardly bend his knees.

"Snow is made out of dog and cat pee," says Peter.

Emily picks her way through the kitchen and looks into the empty living room.

"Okay. You got everything?"

"Jeremy forgot his cap."

"My cappie," moans Jeremy.

"Guys, I'll be back in the morning to say goodbye before I take Karen back to Missoula."

How could it already be over? Beth Anne tries to think what to say, but Pete's already out the door.

"You better get your landlady to fix that window," he calls back over his shoulder. "Looks like somebody tried to take a shot at it."

Then he's gone. Beth Anne listens to his footsteps, all the way down the icy steps, until they come to the end.

Beth Anne can't remember the number of the clinic. She wanders from kitchen to bathroom, knocking over an army of plastic soldiers that had sprung up within minutes of Peter's coming home. A small green soldier on the medicine chest sights along his inch-long rifle at her when she pulls open the mirrored door. She sees she still has plenty of Valium, anyway. She turns and notices more soldiers lined up like insect warriors along the lip of the bathtub. Makes her think of the TV news.

"What are you doing?" asks Emily without looking up from her coloring.

"Looking for the phone book."

Emily is plastering a flattened grocery bag with squares of quivering red and yellow and orange crayon. She lies on her stomach, unseeing, with her nose an inch above her work. A cold sore has made a scabby mess of her upper lip, but the crayon in her hand never falters.

The phone book turns up in the bathroom, after all. Beth Anne picks the soggy cover loose from the gray pages and looks up her own number. Vanago, Mrs. Beth, followed by the same succession of digits that last year's book had said was Vanago, Peter, at the address on Hidden Valley Drive. If she could find last year's book, it would list Vanago, Peter, as though she could go downtown to buy milk and return, not by way of Third Avenue to the apartment, but south up the graveled hill to the short left turn into the driveway.

Noise draws her back into the gray present. The baby sits in the bedroom door, her red mottled face cracking wide open in a squall.

"She needs her pants changed," says Emily. Emily lays down the orange crayon and picks up the yellow one.

Beth Anne remembers that she might have a few clean diapers in the bureau drawer. Everything in the diaper bag has been soiled. She steps over the howling baby and goes to look. Yes, two, three—all threadbare, which was why they'd been left behind when Pete came for the kids before Christmas.

The baby is bundled in so many layers of clothing that only her howls and her stench testify to a living core of flesh and bone. Beth Anne picks loose the soggy knot of the cap and peels it back. The coat is padded and expensive, a miniature ski jacket. Beth Anne fumbles with the zipper until it comes unstuck and looses the full blast of sour milk and drool and ammonia.

The baby lies on her back with her legs sprawled. She's stopped crying. Beth Anne squints against the powerful urine fumes, pulls down the stinking new yellow corduroys, and unpins the diaper.

Without her clothes, the baby seems far less bulky. Her pot belly and her head with its sweat-dampened tendrils are the biggest part of her. Her arms are limp and tender, and so are her legs, and her female fold is swollen and red. Large white blisters have risen between her legs and broken into purplish raw patches. Beth Anne can't remember that her baby ever looked or smelled like this. She looks up, catches Emily watching her.

"Karen. What's she like?"

Emily returns to her artwork. She layers the orange squares on the brown paper bag with more strokes of peeling yellow crayon. "Nice," she says.

"What about the way Caroline smells?" Beth Anne argues. Her eyes smart from the ammonia fumes, and she realizes too late that her voice is louder than she intended. The racket in the kitchen has died, the two boys are watching her from the kitchen door.

Emily mumbles something with her face buried in her coloring.

"I can't hear you!"

Emily chokes, and Beth Anne sees that her face is tear-soaked against the peeling layers of crayon-work. She wishes she knew how to make her voice calm so she could explain to Emily that she only wants to know what Pete and Karen had done to her and Peter and Jeremy and the baby. But what comes out is much worse.

"Why don't they keep you if they know so much?"

The sobs tear out of Emily. "I guess because the boys fought so much, and I—first, when he kept saying he ought to take you to court, I thought he wanted to keep us, but then . . ."

Beth Anne glances back at the baby, who lies with her head rolled slightly to look at nothing while she waits for someone to finish diapering her. One bluish hand slowly closes and uncloses. Beth Anne wishes she could remember birthing her. Emily she can remember birthing, fairly well, although she thinks she might have mixed up that first trip to the hospital with some of the other times. Pete had driven her to the hospital the first time and some of the other times, although at least once her mother had had to drive her.

Emily, she prompts herself. Emily, Peter, Jeremy, Caroline.

Emily Peter Jeremy Caroline Emily Peter Jeremy Caroline Emilypeterjeremycarolineemilypeterjeremycaroline.

Her feet have gone to sleep, and she has to catch herself against the door when she stands up. The shooting pains reach her knees. The boys get out of her way in a hurry as she recovers her balance and limps around the kitchen, looking for the phone book. There it is, she'd carried it out of the bathroom and left it on a chair. The lists of names swim on the gray pages, and it takes several minutes before she can focus and read the number she wants. Reciting the digits to herself, she drops the phone book and dials.

She listens to it ringing and ringing on the other end. Ringing and ringing. Embarrassed, she lowers the receiver. Of course. It's Christmas Day. The clinic is closed.

She searches the book for Dr. Blanton's number and dials it. This time the phone is snatched up on the third ring.

"Dr. Blanton's residence!"

"Um," says Beth Anne, caught off guard. "Can I talk to Dr. Blanton?"

"May I ask who's calling?"

"Beth Anne Connell. I mean, Beth Anne Vanago."

The woman sighs.

"Vanago," Beth Anne says hastily. "I'm a patient of his." She starts to explain how long she has been a patient of his, but the doctor's wife cuts her off.

"It's Christmas Day," she says. "Oh, well, just a minute."

Beth Anne counts the throbs in her feet until, abruptly, the phone is snatched up.

"Blanton!"

The testiness in his voice rattles her. She's bothering the busy doctor. But she sticks to it. "This is Beth Anne Vanago. You know my Valium prescription?"

"Oh. Beth. My wife gave me a different name. What's the matter, did you run out?"

"No. What I want to know is, will Valium kill my kids?"

"What?" he says, startled. "No, Valium won't kill them. What do you mean? You aren't leaving the prescription around where they can play with it, are you?"

"No, I just wondered—"

"The worst Valium'll do is put them to sleep. But you aren't leaving it where they can get into it, are you?"

"No."

"Well, okay, then. Listen, honey," he says, a trifle more patiently. "Those pills helping you to relax?"

"Yes."

"Fine. Oh, Beth Anne, one thing. You aren't drinking any alcoholic beverages, are you?"

"No," she lies.

"Because those pills will double the effects of a drink. You remember that. And you call me if it doesn't seem to you that they're doing the job."

She listens for a moment while the phone buzzes in her ear, but there's no more. The doctor has hung up.

She hangs up, too, and wanders into her bedroom to look for the Valium, stepping over Emily only to come up against the row of pictures strung along the top of the dresser. Four children in artificial ice cream colors. Her feet throb and throb. She supposes she should have asked the doctor about her feet.

The Valium, she reminds herself. It's not in the bedroom, it's in the bathroom medicine cabinet. She limps back through the hall and opens the mirrored door to find the new prescription where she left it, sealed in its clean drugstore envelope.

She sits down on the edge of the bathtub, knocking over a whole army-ant battalion of plastic soldiers, and examines the contents. The plastic bottle has a childproof cap, and she has to squint to line up the arrows before she can pop it loose. She pulls out the wad of cotton and pours some of the pills into her hand.

She's surprised at how small they are, smaller than she remembered. Slick and flat, easy to slide down. Even so, the baby will never be able to swallow them. Probably Jeremy can't, either.

Carefully she funnels all the little pills back into the bottle and carries the bottle out to the kitchen, where she lays a square of paper towel on the table and pours out the pills to divide them into four equal heaps.

19

She leads the pack. Although she's smaller than her littermates and the younger pup, she's been the alpha female since birth. A snap from her is usually enough to send her brothers fawning. Now she breaks off her frisking and trots off at a steady pace through the sagebrush, taking advantage of every shadow and hollow of ground. Only a nighthawk or a human eye trained to pick out life could see her or the other coyotes, and a human eye probably couldn't do it at midnight. The pack comes close to being invisible in their invisible world, like a reminder that all is not on the surface.

At the top of the low bluff above the sheep sheds, the young coyote pauses. A quick human eye might make out her silhouette briefly as she slides across the trail between one outcropping and another and crouches, intent on the human domain below her. Her ears twitch, her nostrils twitch, her fine senses pick up a host of messages untranslatable into any language.

No dog strains or whines at the end of a chain down there, which of course she already knows. But something is new from last night. The smell of ponderous domestic bodies enshrouded in wool and bedded down like pale boulders waiting for snowfall. The smell of warm blood and flesh is also the smell of the forbidden, and she is fixed upon it.

20

Being pregnant she remembers as, at first, not having a period, in itself a not unpleasant symptom once the doctor had confirmed the worst. But then her legs began to ache. During the wedding ceremony they ached in the support hose her mother had bought her until the main thing on her mind was not Pete's face, washed-out as the stalks of narcissi, but only how soon the pastor would get it over with so she could sit down. Worst of all was the pain in her inner thighs, right up against her groin where the support hose couldn't help. A varicose vein, her mother said, and it hurt day and night.

You never want to! Pete accused her the second time she said her legs hurt when she spread them. She choked and lay as still as she could on her side of the new king-size bed, and when Pete's hand came to rest on her buttocks, she thought it meant he wasn't angry. But soon the hand began to explore, pushing under the elastic legs of her pajamas to work its way deeper, tentatively at first as though it didn't know what it would find, then jabbing with urgency. She began to cry.

Shit! Pete exploded out of bed, hurling back the covers. She heard him pulling on his pants.

Where are you going.

You don't have to know that, he said, and she understood from his tone that he had just scored a point against her.

Her body continued to change in ways she never could have surmised before her pregnancy. With fascinated horror she watched the heavy blue veins squirm to the surface of her breasts while her nipples spread and darkened. She had had pretty nipples. Now she held a hand mirror to see how they covered the ends of her breasts, ugly, with lumps and puckers that made them look like something to suck.

In the late mornings she stood in front of the full length mirror, checking her belly for signs of growth. A watched pot wouldn't boil. Still, her belly had stretched out the bottoms of her panties before she noticed a change. From then on she could notice nothing else. Her belly continued to grow like a thing apart from the rest of her body. Stretch marks like bluish-white worms sprang up across the growth. She ran an experimental finger down one of the stretch marks and felt the sensation of her belly splitting like a parting zipper.

But the most unexpected and grotesque change of all was when her navel popped out of its comfortable little depression to protrude from her belly like a sore little nose, as painful as her nipples when she accidentally brushed against it. She thought the ruptured navel, poking inquisitively through her new maternity clothes, was the ugliest of all the changes in her body. Every high school girl knew that sex with the boy she loved would change everything. Looking at her navel in the mirror, Beth Anne understood why nobody ever told them exactly what would change.

* * *

Now she sits in a dirty kitchen on the other side of town from Hidden Valley Drive. Remembering how small the baby is, she removes several pills from one heap and divides them among the other three heaps. Working carefully to keep stray pills from hopping off the counter on the floor, she pounds them into powder with the back of a cleaver.

When she finishes, she takes down the mugs. And yes, she has remembered to buy milk. She pours each mug almost full and then adds to each its portion of the crushed Valium, which is a mistake. The powder floats on the surface and refuses to dissolve. She finds a clean spoon and stirs, but the granules stick to the spoon and have to be wiped off with her fingers.

The pregnancy went on and on. Her stomach grew until she thought she surely couldn't grow bigger. But she did. She's so big for seven months, her mother marveled to her women friends in front of Beth Anne. When they were alone she questioned her anxiously about her diet. How much do you eat, honey? All that weight has to come off afterward you know.

She thought her skin might split from the growth. She noted how she was beginning to tilt back and arch her spine to off-set her changing center of gravity. One whole day she ate nothing and still her stomach grew. She began to realize that nothing would stop it.

Pete didn't want her to be seen outside the house. How come, she pressed when she realized something lay behind his re-luctance to take her to a movie or out for a beer with his football buddies and their current girls.

You want everybody to see you're that way! he finally yelled in exasperation.

She remembered that in high school being pregnant meant that you had been doing it and now everybody knew. In spite of the doctor's reassurances, she began to realize there was some-thing nasty about her condition.

* * *

She stands, wincing as her feet squish under her weight. The apartment has grown dead quiet. She goes to the door of the living room and sees that the baby has gone to sleep on the floor with her diaper still unpinned and her corduroys unsnapped.

Emily crouches on the floor under the arm of the couch, hugging her knees and looking at nothing. The disemboweled grocery bag is spread in the middle of the floor under the wreckage of Emily's crayons, its thick dizzying colors straining as though to escape.

"Where are the boys?"

"I'n know."

She looks into the smaller bedroom. A tiny sound catches her attention, and she lifts up the trailing blanket from the bed.

"What are you doing under there?"

Jeremy whimpers, but Peter says, "Playing."

She reaches under the bed and catches a foot. Jeremy's, she thinks. The new blue and white tennis shoe seems heavy and much larger than her baby's feet would wear, but she tugs, and out slides Jeremy along with the blanket and several rolls of dust.

"Playing what?"

"Cave."

"Well, come out. I want you to drink some milk."

She expects them to argue, but even Peter comes along to the kitchen without a murmur. Even Emily comes quietly to the table.

"I don't like this milk," says Emily when she tastes hers, but her voice is small, and after a moment she swallows.

Beth Anne goes to get the baby. She hesitates a moment over the small sleeping nugget, limp as a rag doll in her disheveled clothing. It seems a shame to wake her to drink her dose, but what if her sleep is not sound enough without it? When she picks her up, the baby's head lolls on her shoulder, but then she rouses and frets a little from the pain of her diaper rash.

"Don't cry. It won't hurt long," Beth Anne counsels her. But she feels a surge of anger. New clothes on the outside, sores underneath. Surely her baby never had such sores.

She props the baby on her lap and holds the mug for her. The baby's eyelids rise and sink. She takes a little milk in her mouth and lets it dribble out the corner, but Beth Anne is patient, and she presses the mug on her again.

At first she thought she had eaten something that disagreed with her. All morning it gnawed away at her stomach until she couldn't sit still. It was not until four in the afternoon when, sitting on the toilet with her mottled stomach resting on her thighs and her maternity slacks down around her ankles, she happened to look down and see the stain of blood in the crotch of her panties.

Getting sick, the women called it.

How will I know when it starts, she had asked her mother.

You'll know, all right, said her mother with a sharp little laugh, and Beth Anne was left to patch together half-remembered conversations among her mother's friends with snippets from novels or movies about boiling plenty of water and expecting pains every three minutes.

Oh god yes, said her mother when she finally came to the phone after a long wait until she could get rid of a customer. You've started.

I have!

Her first reaction was pure delight that it wasn't another cramp or muscle twitch. It was coming to an end, she was going to be normal again.

You'll change that tune before the night's over, said her mother grimly. And where's Pete?

He's—she thought as fast as she could. If he's out with the beer truck there's no way to get hold of him. Lots of times he comes home about seven.

Seven was when his friends quit drinking and went home for supper.

I'll find him, said her mother.

She wandered about the house, looking out the front window for her mother's car or Pete's in the driveway. Her legs felt heavy, and her breasts and the heavy stomach dragged at her. The growth had knotted like a clenched fist, and the varicose vein in her thigh throbbed, but she could not sit down. The gnaw of discomfort was getting hungrier. Nothing, she realized with the first touch of panic, would stop it.

Would it hurt? Of course she knew it would hurt, just as she knew that holding the baby afterward made it all worthwhile, but would it really really hurt, more than she could stand?

At last she saw her mother's car pull into the driveway. Her mother, still in the four-inch heels and pale green suit she had worn to work, was getting out from behind the wheel. Pete, looking cross, got out of the passenger's side. Beth Anne knew he hated to ride in a car that somebody else was driving.

Her mother clattered in. Where's your suitcase, what do you mean you haven't packed yet? Use this, she said, dragging the blue weekender from the matching set out of the closet, and under her direction Beth Anne took cosmetics and underthings out of drawers and packed them with nightgowns and slippers and one of her old school skirts and a sweater to wear home.

If they'll still *fit!* Now honey, don't drag so. Pete wants to take you to the hospital now so he can eat supper before it gets too late.

You're not coming?

Honey, it isn't like there's anything I can do. I'll be up tomorrow to see you and the baby.

Tomorrow was another eon. But her mother was pushing her out the door, and Pete, who had been hanging around, came to carry the suitcase.

I have a dinner date, her mother was explaining to Pete. You can reach me if it's really necessary. But it probably won't be. They'll probably send you home as soon as you sign her in.

The snowless winter afternoon was gathering gloom as Pete turned on the headlights of her mother's car and turned on the street to the hospital when ummph! The pain startled the grunt out of her. She couldn't have told anyone else what it felt like, but it really really hurt. She looked wildly at Pete.

Take it easy he advised with his eyes on the stoplight. When he turned up the long stone-edged driveway to the night entrance, the globe lights glowed and Beth Anne's feet were jammed against the floor. Her belly was rigid.

Ummph! It took her breath away.

Oh jesuschrist!

But it hurts!

You can't—oh for chrissake! But Pete was trembling as he found a place to park her mother's car and got her suitcase out of the back seat and carried it for her up the long flight of stone steps. He waited in the hall with his hands in his pockets while Beth Anne tried to think of answers to all the questions the night nurse asked.

Through here. Another nurse took her arm and Beth Anne allowed herself to be led into a large, brilliantly lit room with several stirruped examination tables and a row of doorless toilets.

Sign this. It's a receipt for your watch and wedding ring.

She scrawled her name, remembering to write Vanago instead of Connell, and watched as the nurse dropped her jewelry into a brown envelope and sealed it.

Get into this.

She took the folded white cotton, which turned out to be a hospital gown, starched and split up the back. She turned to ask where Pete was, but the nurse already had vanished through the swinging doors, so she got undressed, fumbling with her buttons and gasping at the pain. The gown hit her at knee-level. Her stomach protruded so far in front that the gown gaped in back and exposed her buttocks.

The nurse materialized through the doors with a tray of equipment. Get up on the table. You're one of Dr. Blanton's, right?

Where's Pete, I mean, my husband.

He can't come in here. You've got to be prepped. Here, feet in the stirrups.

Beth Anne felt her crotch being bathed with something warm. The nurse selected a tool from her tray. Unexpectedly, something bit Beth Anne, and she yelped.

Sorry. I'll get a new blade.

The bright overhead lights burned at her sockets even when she screwed her eyes shut. She gritted her teeth and bore the weight of her stomach while the razor scraped across her privates. She longed to arch her back to relieve the ache, but she feared the nurse's annoyance.

The nurse dropped something into a jar. Over on your side now and draw up your knees.

She obeyed awkwardly. At first it was a relief to support her belly on the examination table. It had been months since she could sleep comfortably on her back. But she had caught a glimpse of the nurse donning yellow gloves, wheeling something behind her. She stiffened as a finger, laden with grease, probed her anus.

Hold still!

She dug her fingernails into her palms, but still she clenched her muscles when a still, cold tube began to penetrate her.

It'll be over as soon as you relax!

She felt fingers spread her buttocks apart, felt the cold tube slide in. She began to cry. She wanted to kick, but she couldn't seem to make her legs move. The nurse reached up and did something to an overhead valve. There was a gush, and Beth Anne felt herself filling with something warm and wet, at first not unpleasant, but insistent, filling her so full that she knew she couldn't hold more.

That's enough! she pleaded. Please! she wept, but the merciless flow continued.

With no more warning than it had entered, the tube retracted. As it did, the nurse's fingers clamped Beth Anne's buttocks together, hard. Just another minute while it does its job!

She lay under the inexorable lights, afraid to breathe and afraid to move. She could feel the paper-covered pad under her cheek and see the stainless steel bar six inches from her face. Beyond was a tiled wall. The lights burned.

Just as she thought she would always be suspended between containing the enema for the rest of time and bursting with it, the nurse released her. She rolled off the table and tried to run on her rubber legs for a toilet cubicle. Just in time she made it, with the gown parting behind her and her bowels collapsing into the bowl with a gush of broken feces and soapsuds. She leaned over her stomach to rest her face on her knees and weep exhausted tears until the rigidity of her womb forced her to sit up straight.

She saw her legs, white and inadequate under the bulge of her belly. She saw her feet, gray under the toenails, planted on the damp tile in front of the toilet. As she sat dripping soapy water and staring at her feet, it seemed to Beth Anne that she had come to the end of an inhuman process that no one had warned her would seize her and refuse to let her go until it had reduced her to this quivering, ugly hulk. Who would believe that this swollen belly, with its spidery legs and its stench, had ever been frosted in white tulle and taken to a prom?

Don't wipe!

The nurse was urging her off the toilet. Beth Anne remembered that she was having a baby. Dripping, wobbling under the nurse's guidance, she climbed up on the table. A pain gripped her, and she clutched at the nurse.

You've still got a long wait, said the nurse. No, no! Lay on your back!

But it's so heavy.

All the same, that's how you got to lay.

Beth Anne settled back under the weight of her belly and waited. The lights stung her eyes, so she put up her hand and watched the lines of glowing red between her fingers until her arm began to ache and she let it fall.

The labor room door stayed shut. She began to hear the sounds of the hospital. Rubber wheels passing rapidly in the hall. A doctor being paged, far away. Her belly weighed painfully against her vitals. She looked for her watch to see how much time had passed and remembered that the nurse had taken it away.

A giant pain gripped her without warning and squeezed until she could not breathe. Terrified, Beth Anne fought for air while the overhead lights danced with blue and purple spots and the pain bore down and ground her with the weight of the world. The room rumbled. Just as she thought she would suffocate, the pain eased and she nearly choked on a great draft of breath. She began to cry.

The doors swung open. Daddy, you might as well go home and have a good night's sleep. Nothing's going to happen before morning.

Pete! She grabbed at him.

He pried her fingers loose. You heard her. It isn't like I can do anything.

She tried to explain how frightening it was to be all by herself in the big brilliant room, and how much it would help if somebody stayed with her, even if they couldn't do anything, but the pain seized her again and squeezed and turned the room purple. Pete freed himself and vanished. The pain ground on and on before it left her panting.

I can't stand this! she screamed when she got her breath.

The nurse appeared from somewhere and swabbed her hip. Beth Anne received the hypodermic joyfully. As her legs numbed, she was able to lie back on the paper-covered pad and let her tears dry while the pains came and went through a growling distance. Thunder, she thought. Rain. She felt so hot. She wished she could get out from under the heavy hospital gown. Somewhere a telephone was ringing. A rubber-wheeled cart passed in the hall with another woman's sobs—owee, owee, like a small child's.

Then, as she drowsed, another pain took her by surprise and crunched down with all the force it had, and more. Beth Anne struggled, but she knew it wasn't going to stop until it had split her apart. Then it ebbed, and she yelled while she had the chance, because another contraction was following right behind it.

The nurse was saying something from between her legs.

It hurts! Beth Anne howled, and the nurse said something about not daring another shot for thirty minutes, but Beth Anne soon lost track because another pain had hit her. Mommy! she screamed, because surely her mother would come and get her, because this was a mistake, because surely nobody could withstand what was happening to her.

Women were talking in the room.

Any coffee left?

No, a slow night, only two. This one's been screaming her head off.

A strange nurse was administering something to her hindquarters. Okay! she called. The rumbling cart was coming through the swinging doors, lining up beside her. Hands guided Beth Anne from table to cart. Then she was rolling through a corridor and into a second brilliantly lit room where, through high eastern windows, the night was beginning to pale.

She was being moved off the cart to another table. At first she settled back, distracted from her terror by all the activity, but then she jerked away. One of her wrists had been strapped to the table, her knees were being strapped apart. She saw her feet, waggling helplessly in the air. She fought, but her other wrist was being strapped down, and she knew they were going to tear her to pieces. Already she was being split lengthwise at the crotch.

Gas? somebody said.

Not yet.

Bear down, somebody said.

Now the gas.

Something was being fitted over her face, hot rubber with an alien smell.

Take a deep breath, said somebody, and Beth Anne took a cautious taste and then, as the gas came rushing with its velvet relief, she sucked as hard as she could at the depths of unconsciousness and an end of her ordeal. It was not until the next afternoon when she had been washed and sewn up and had slept off the gas that they brought the baby up from the nursery and told her it was hers.

21

The young replacement ewes are bedded down on the south slope of the pasture for the night. Suddenly they jerk awake as one, stumbling and bleating out of the warm imprints of their bodies as the coyote pack sweeps down upon them. Bound by their instinct to herd together, the ewes wash in a futile tide down the pasture slope toward the dirt road where, the day before, they had been herded after most of their band had been sorted and tallied and loaded on trucks bound for the annual sheep auction in Billings. But the shadows are there to cut them off.

Working like a trained pack, the coyotes drive the panicky ewes back and forth in waves toward the lower corner of the pasture. The only sounds come from the ewes themselves. The miniature thunder of their hooves, their shortwinded gasps, the scream when a sheep on the outer fringe is brought down by jaws tearing at its wool. Staples screech as the first wave hits the woven wire fence. Heads jerk back, leg bones snap. Driven by the dumbness of their kind and by their terror of the coyotes, the rest of the flock pile against and on top of their downed leaders.

A pair of coyotes drag a smoking carcass off through the snow, snarling and tearing through the wool to get at the vitals. A hundred yards away a bleeding straggler stumbles toward the carnage, even in its extremity drawn by its herd instinct back into destruction. The coyotes work on the quivering mass of bleeding ewes, snapping and tearing wherever they can find throat or belly. Gradually the flock becomes a pile of bloody wool packed against the fence. Movement at the bottom of the pile is spasmodic.

Pity?

22

She waits for a long time in the kitchen of the silent apartment and watches the shadow of the cottonwood twigs lengthen across the snowy window ledge and merge into the approaching dusk. With nightfall more snow begins to fall.

At last she gropes her way through the strewn toys and clothing in the near darkness. She hears only regular breathing from the small shapes on the couch. Through the hall and into the bedroom, avoiding the bedroom dresser and its ghostly faces, she turns on the light just long enough to find her coat and her shoulder bag. The revolver drops into the bag with a satisfying drag.

Has she disturbed the sleeping children? No. The rhythms of their breathing rise and fall as inexorably as the deepening snow. She hesitates. Why not break the pattern now, before it has a chance to grow and swell into pain unendurable?

But no. Pete is the piece that will break the pattern.

Up to her ankles in snow on the landing, she pulls the door firmly shut and listens with her ear against the glass pane, in case the sound of the latch has disturbed the children. But she hears not a sound, and so she locks the door and hobbles down the treacherous steps into the silence of freshly falling snow.

23

Shaken by her close call, she rests her forehead on the steering wheel while snow swirls around her car. Whatever had streaked across the highway in front of her headlights, she had hit her brakes, skidded on fresh snow and freezing slush, overcompensated, and come to rest here on the verge of the borrow pit. What had saved her was no good judgment of her own but the dead weeds from last summer sticking their stalky heads through the snow and providing her tires with enough traction to stop their wild, widening spirals. Will her heart ever slow down? She had come so close, at the very least, to an uncontrolled plunge down the borrow pit into fender-deep snow she could never have ground or spun her way out of. At night on the snowbound prairie, miles from the last ranch yard light, she might have shivered for hours, or worse. She can still feel the steering wheel swinging out of control in her hands, the swerves, the car fantailing on sheer ice. It had been that close.

And another thirty miles to drive, she supposes. At least thirty miles. Trembling, she retrieves her books and briefcase from where they've been catapulted, like expendables in the first moments of the skid, under the dashboard on the passenger side. She's got to do it. That, or sit here all night in the rapidly cooling car. So she starts the ignition and pulls back, slowly and carefully, on the highway.

Keep your mind on what you're doing, she lectures herself. Don't let your thoughts wander. It's too easy to lose it all.

24

Her feet, bloated beyond fitting into any of her shoes, had presented a problem until she thought of wrapping them in towels and pulling her overshoes on over the towels. Now her feet no longer pain her, but they squish and wobble awkwardly under her, and she tires rapidly as she struggles down the unshoveled streets. She scolds herself for stopping at the end of nearly every block to rest, and yet she knows she has to conserve her strength. The Diamond Club, where she thinks Bud will take Pete and Karen for Christmas dinner, lies a mile east of town, beyond the stockyards.

Once out on the east highway, however, she finds that the wind and traffic have beaten the snow to a hard glaze that she can grip with her overshoes, and she makes better time. Soon she recognizes the dark palisades of the stockyards and, beyond the stockyards, the flashing neon of the Diamond Club, which, along with the few snowswept cars huddled close to the entrance of the rambling, low building, reassures her that, even on Christmas night, the club is open.

The Diamond Club had been the fashionable place to come for dinner before proms and parties, back in high school days. Tonight the darkness of the interior is warm and velvety. Panting, she bends over double in the foyer until she can get her breath back and focus her night-blind eyes on the distant points of candlelight, and she tries to remember how the dining room is arranged. Gradually she sees that she's standing at the entrance to the bar where a backlight glitters on rows of bottles against padded red vinyl. One or two indistinct figures huddle over their drinks at the bar.

Through the archway a vast darkened cavern opens, of empty tables and a deserted bandstand. Candles in red or green bowls flicker at the few occupied tables. Not a big night at the Diamond Club. But she can't distinguish the silhouettes of the people around the candles. Either she's going to have to find a waitress and ask her about a Vanago reservation, or else she'll have to walk past every candle to see whose faces it lights.

Her feet throb, and she thinks she might as well rest them and adjust the towels while she decides what to do. The restrooms are on the other side of the bar, and she bumps into chairs and flimsy tables on her way to the door under the lighted sign.

In the women's room she stumps into one of the cubicles and lowers herself heavily. She can't remember when it ever felt so fine to be off her feet. Reaching down awkwardly over her coat and bulky purse, she eases her right foot out of its overshoe. A ripe odor rises as she unwraps the towel.

She pokes at the green and yellow foot, wondering whether she ought to run water over it or what. The throb is more distracting than really painful, so she ends up rewrapping the towel and working the foot back into the overshoe.

She's unwrapping her other foot to have a look when someone runs into the restroom on racketing high heels and locks herself in the next cubicle.

Someone else opens the door. "Julie?"

Silence in the cubicle next to her, then a sniffle.

"Julie, you don't have to wait for him if you aren't feeling well. We can take you home."

Another long pause. Beth Anne's left foot is not quite so puffy as her right one was. She sniffs it and rearranges its towel.

The bolt on the next cubicle slides back. High heels rachet on tile. "Hey, I'm fine! Hey, you weren't worried about me?"

The heels click across the floor, the door closes. Beth Anne waits, sniffing her feet, until she's sure she's alone. Then she wipes her wet forehead with a piece of toilet paper and hoists herself up-right.

Then she stops, her hands jerking, because one of the women still stands at the mirror, combing her hair.

Beth Anne can't help watching. She's never seen such hair. It reaches the other woman's waist, lovely dark brown hair with a soft watery sheen that any man might long to plunge into and re-fresh himself in.

Two wide blue eyes meet hers in the mirror, turn a polite blank.

But suddenly Beth Anne knows who this girl must be. She licks her lips. Because never has she seen such a pretty girl, a girl so luscious and yet so thin that her pelvic bones protrude like two precious ridges beneath her velvety blue jeans. Her long lovely hair falls over a soft dark blue sweater that swells with breasts as small and round and hard as bee stings. Beth Anne is sure that no baby has ever sucked on those breasts.

"It hurts!" she warns. "It really really hurts!"

The other woman hastily drops her comb back into her purse and backs toward the door.

"Nobody else will tell you!" Beth Anne shouts after her, but the door swings shut, and Beth Anne is alone in the bright overhead light that reflects off the scabby tiles and the mirror.

Then she remembers that this woman will lead her to Pete. With her overshoes flopping, Beth Anne hobbles after her as fast as she can.

Tinsel from the archway catches in the girl's long hair and casts a startled halo as she glances back and then bolts into the unlit cavern. Beth Anne ducks under the tinsel and follows her. She has no difficulty at all in keeping her in sight. And there is Pete with a red candle glowing on his face and highlighting his fair hair. His expression when he looks up and sees Beth Anne reminds her of the Juneau girls. And she hasn't even taken her revolver out of her shoulder bag.

A waitress trots up with a pot of coffee, begins, "Are you ready to order now—" and takes a startled step backward with the coffee sloshing in the pot. Julie Burchette with her wizened little face, Bud with his bald head. The table tipping. Beth Anne thinks they all look as though they're trying to keep their balance on a sinking floor.

Pete gasps. Beth Anne looks to see if he's really seeing her, and he is. She leans down and squints to make sure, and what she sees in his eyes is the tiny flame of the candle, diminished a thousand times, and beyond the candle flame are all the dark nothings she has ever dreaded.

Pete's mouth moves. Fascinated, she watches the crawl of his facial muscles as he shapes words. Realizes that she can hear what he is saying.

"The kids. What have you done with the kids?"

If he's addressing her, she must not quite be invisible. She's not nothing yet. She draws just enough breath to answer him.

"Asleep."

"Alone?" He's on his feet, his voice booming. "Alone? Alone? Alone?"

"Asleep," she repeats. She mouths the sounds. Only a lip's twitch of difference. Asleep. Alone. Asleep. Alone.

Fingers grip her through her coat sleeve, and she grabs for her shoulder bag.

"Go home. Go home. Stay with them tonight. I'll come for them in the morning."

Go home. Go home. Asleep. Alone.

"No," she said. "You won't."

You won't. Go home. Asleep. Alone.

But she's being drawn away. This too occurred previously on the squirrel wheel of the past few days, but she can't remember where or when. She sees the candlelight recede before she remembers why she came. She attempts language one last time.

"This is your last chance!" she shouts.

The bar lights spin past her. She recognizes a face, or at least a black hat. It's the shotgun man, he's sitting at the bar with a woman in a dark red sweater. He seems to turn up everywhere, like bad luck. She starts to warn the shotgun man to stop following her, but she's beyond words now, and anyway the door of the Diamond Club is opening on frozen air and she's being pushed out into the parking lot where snowflakes float down on silent cars.

"You got a car?"

Beth Anne looks around to see who is booming at her. The bouncer, she guesses. He wears a white shirt that turns eerie when he stands under the neon.

Boom. Boom. You got a car. Home. Alone.

But she must have shaken her head, because the bouncer adds, "What's the matter with you, bothering people? You wait a minute and I'll get somebody to drive you home."

Left alone, she lets her feet carry her toward the highway. The night clouds bear a faint pink reflection from the lights of Versailles, the posts of the stockyards loom up out of the dark. Nothing is north of the stockyards, nothing but thirty empty miles and then the Canadian prairie. She looks up and down the highway, but no lights are in sight, and she makes her dash across open pavement as fast as her feet are able. Once in the shadows of the palisades, she stops for breath and catches a whiff of warm animal scent.

25

The coyote pack withdraws with their zest satiated and their stomachs packed with the bowels and vitals of the three or four ewes they bothered to drag away from the pileup. Like shadows they disperse to the coulees and secret crevices of their holdings, and nothing moves in their wake.

26

She squats in the shelter of the board gate. Behind her the dozen calves huddle together in the lee corner of their pen. At first they had snuffed and stamped, but gradually they have lost interest in her. The wind ruffles their heavy coats, and fingers of blowing, drifting snow stretch across the highway toward the low concrete-block building under the neon Diamond sign.

In the beginning its door had opened and shut often, spilling out light. Men had come out in their shirtsleeves and shone lights in the parked cars, and somebody had jumped in a truck and driven west toward town. She had watched between the cracks in the gate as the truck roared by. Gradually silence had returned.

Now, as she watches, the Diamond sign is turned off. It lingers as a glow on the back of her eyes, then fades to nothing. She shivers. She still knows the difference between hot and cold, although the numbness in her feet has crept upward and claimed her lower extremities. She'd like to cram herself into the corner of the pen with the calves. She'd absorb their body heat. Grow a shaggy winter pelt of her own. But part of her still remembers that Pete had said to go home. After awhile she unbars the gate and lets herself out on the highway.

27

Doubling back, the coyote dives frantically for the shelter of a clump of snow-choked sagebrush, but the plane cuts her off, and she reverses and scrabbles for the coulee. But the coulee is too far away, she's trapped in open snow. For an instant she stands at bay, plume stiffened and forelegs braced, as she lifts her head and snarls defiance at the plane.

28

She slinks out of the shadows. As far as she can see, she's alone except for a traffic light suspended above the snowpacked street, blinking red and yellow. She tastes the change in the weather. The coyote hunter was right, the storm has blown through northern Montana. A few stray flakes rise from rooftops, spin in the streetlights and settle down into the chill blanket that has transformed the street and the empty parking lots and the dim cars and windowless buildings into a pristine world of soft unbroken white.

A truck roars up, and she flattens herself back against a brick wall, into a recess that was once a window. Somebody jumps out of the truck and scans the street. Black hat, shotgun man, drawn to trouble like a crow to roadkill. He's calling out, because a drift of wind carries his human voice, indistinct and disintegrating into the insulating layers of snow, as far as her ears. But language is nothing to her now. Her feet, which dimly she remembers had burned her in their agony, have now lost all feeling.

The truck pulls away. She hears nothing more, nothing moves in the street, and yet she fears to leave the safety of the recess and expose herself against the snow. And when she finally ventures out, headlights send her cowering back, not into a doorway this time, but against a row of garbage cans on a platform by a dead lilac hedge. Twigs thrust through her coat and and try to claim her, but she crashes through the blackened branches until she finds a little hollow where the snow has drifted into a kind of nest. Crouching down in this precarious sanctuary, she watches the street.

A black and white patrol car eases along, its dome light shut down and its engine hardly louder than the crunch of its tires through eight inches of fresh snow. She dares not breathe. Within the darkened car she can make out two visored heads. One of the heads is speaking into a small dark box he holds in his hand. Then the patrol car eases on past her and continues east until its head-lights are absorbed by the night.

29

Just as daylight breaks, the rancher leaves the kitchen and pauses on the doorstep to light a cigarette. The match warms his face briefly before it flickers out. He notes the change in the weather as he drops the spent match in the snow at his feet. A warm wind is blowing from the west, a chinook wind that carries warm air over the Rocky Mountains from the Pacific and dumps it on the plains. As the rancher starts down toward the sheds to fire up the tractor and feed the ewes, he thinks that the great snowfields already are shrinking from the sudden rise in temperature. Then he happens to notice the strange whitish pile, like a misplaced hill, in the lower corner of the sheep pasture. At first he doesn't know what he's seeing.

30

She squats cautiously in the wild patterns cast on the snow by the wind-whipped cottonwood twigs. The warm wind howls in the high branches, drives garbage cans rattling, laves her face. She can smell rotting leaves. By dawn the chinook will have softened the snow, by nightfall it will have lain bare the trash and jetsam of Versailles.

When she thinks it's safe, she steals through the wind-whipped shadows of branches and creeps up the steps at the side of the house. Rapidly melting snow has packed and caked under her disintegrating feet, and she almost slips and falls. When she reaches the landing, she pauses where branches lash at the side of the house and sniffs the wind that whines against the eaves and sets water dripping off the shingles. To the north the obscure roofs of Versailles lead all the way down to the river. Beyond the river, the blowing line of bluffs gradually materializes out of the paling night sky.

Below the landing, in a yard across the street, a small evergreen strung with Christmas lights casts its colored strings to the wind and dances like a frantic thing, as if it's trying to free itself from its roots and dance away.

She's sure no one could have seen or heard her approach the house, and yet she turns the knob so slowly and silently that no watcher might have distinguished movement. The door inches ajar. She looks one last time down the street with its shrinking snow and writhing, tortured trees before she drags herself over the threshold into her own rank, airless space.

Her eyes slowly adjust until the dark humps and shapes become familiar. The smell is her own smell. But still she waits, ears pricked in the dark, until gradually she picks up the rhythm of breathing.

All is just as she left it. But slowly she pads through the familiar, stinking rubble from room to room, sniffing each small warm shape as she comes to it. Their smell is hers and yet alien. She knows the den has been fouled.

The telephone rings. It rings and rings and rings again, and she cringes back and listens to the frightful sound.

31

After a few miles she's still trembling and reliving her loss of control, she's gripping the steering wheel as if she expects it to try to get away, but she's driving west into an increasingly erratic headwind that howls and whips at her car. She realizes with relief that she's beginning to make out objects in the car. And yes, landscape is returning with the first gray light. An eroded line of buttes. Fence posts cutting across shrunken snow, wet weeds hanging on by their roots in the force of the wind.

She shudders. If her skid had sent her spiraling even a little farther, no one would have known for hours. Days even. Disconnected from family, a thousand miles from friends in Illinois, a dean in Versailles known to her only through long distance telephone lines, how long before she would have been missed? For the first time she understands the significance of the expression *losing touch*. She's come so close. What if she had let her fantasies run wild. She might be orbiting the moon on a lone track by now. In her shaky state, she's near to tears when she thinks about all the orbits of the disconnected, all the solitary stories, all the narratives that never touch. Trembling from the physical memory of her wild spin, regretting the arrogance of her young years, she resolves that she will never again lose touch.

32

Remembering that she knows how to count. Eight. Nine. Ten. Eleven. Twelve. The act of counting draws her back from the shadow realm, and she remembers other human tasks that she has left undone.

The telephone stops ringing. The absence of sound seems almost as violent as sound.

When she's sure it's done ringing, she crawls over to it and picks up the receiver. Fumbles with the dial.

"Operator."

"I want the police station."

"You can dial that number directly."

Somewhere in the shadowy apartment, a child sighs deeply in its sleep.

"Do you need help?"

But still she says nothing, and after a moment she hears the telephone ringing on the other end, and then a woman's voice.

"Police, may I help you?"

"I want to talk to the coyote hunter."

"Who's speaking?"

She remembers a name. "Beth Anne Connell, I mean Vanago. She's going to kill her kids."

She repeats her street address out of habit and replaces the receiver on a jangle of protest on the other end. Relieved at having completed all human assignments, she resumes her silent patrol of the apartment until the windows begin to take form as oblongs of frosted gray. It's nearly morning.

33

So what does she hope to find in Versailles?

Like any small town, the dean had said, except that Versailles started out as a railhead camp, and some argue that it still retains the, well, frontier spirit, one might call it. Vigor. Violence, even. And of course there are the Indian reservations, we've got one to the west and one to the south of us. Lot of poverty out there, alcoholism, unemployment. We try to get the younger ones enrolled in college classes, but it's hard.

But it's always what you make of it, he said. We have the good and the bad. Heroism, even. We had a young man, a year ago now, well, mercy flight in a private plane, crashed, crippled for life. Well, it's a long story. And it's true, the isolation out here does strange things to people.

And she had thought, well, she'd always been independent. She'd always walked by herself. She had thought that living for a few years at the rim of the prairie would at least afford her privacy. She would have time for her own research, time to write herself out of the place and into the kind of job that she merited.

34

She shudders at the touch of metal, but the gun is what she's got. She manages to balance herself upright on her mutilated feet, she raises the revolver to the height of her shoulders and grips it in both hands. A shadow materializes between her and the gray window, and she bares her teeth. It's the shotgun man.

"Shoot me if you gotta shoot somebody," he says. And he takes the one step.

She had expected the thunder of the revolver, but not, in the half-light of dawn, its lightning flash, and she draws back in fear. Then all lights come on at once, and she crouches and aims the gun. But the coyote hunter has burst in with companions in dark blue and silver uniforms that seem to be everywhere, and she dithers, not knowing which to fire on first. The coyote hunter takes the gun from her hand. Jesuschrist, he says. He walks around her and stops in the doorway. Jake, he says.

35

Now she thinks, she'll find peace and quiet, yes, but she also thinks, she'll find friends. She almost but won't quite let herself think, she'll find love. She thinks, with time, she'll find a way to weave some threads together.

Les Belles Dames Sans Merci

"You are the last person I ever expected to see here," says the woman on the next barstool. "The very last."

Her clever eyes search Jen's face, not as other women's eyes during this weekend have searched for wrinkles and sagging chin to compare with the decay of their own faces, but as if for a revelation.

Jen remembers her now. In high school she was the hick from the sticks, whereas Jen herself had been a townie. But this woman had been a smart hick, top grades and a scholarship. And clotheswise at least, she's still smart. She's wearing pressed Calvin Klein blue jeans that show off her sixty-year-old butt and a silk shirt she doesn't seem to care is soaking up spilled liquor where her elbow rests on the bar. Her name suddenly surfaces from Jen's back brain. Laura.

"Yes, well, don't ask me why I came," says Jen.

"Jeanette—"

"Jen. Everyone calls me Jen now."

"Jen. We were so *horrible* to you in high school. Listen, we can have one more, can't we? The banquet's going to be late, nobody's leaving the bar yet."

"Sure, why not," says Jen. What she remembers is being horrible to Laura in high school, but maybe Laura's memories are kinder to herself.

It's July, and the bartender has propped open the door of the American Legion Hall to let out the cigarette smoke and hope for a breeze. He's a young fellow, with big shoulders and a mustache and hair grown shaggy over his ears. Jen thinks he looks familiar, but maybe it's just his type that she's recognizing. She hardly knows a soul in town anymore. From where she sits at the bar, she can see a slice of white-hot parking lot and four lanes of highway curving down to what used to be called Main Street Hill, and, across the highway, dry grass and an eight-foot fence behind which two buffalo cows and a calf wait for sundown. As Jen watches, a car with out-of-state plates slows and a window slides down so the kids in the back seat can get a look at real wildlife.

She remembers Main Street as she supposes others in the class of '57 do. She remembers huddling under Richard's arm as they cruised in his father's Chrysler, laved by the headlights of other cruising cars, up and down between the lighted A&W at the top of Main Street Hill and the lighted Dash-In at the bottom, and the streams of horn blasts as high school pairs acknowledged other pairs, the vibration of the car, and air from the heater under the hem of her skirt, and the radio playing rock and roll on a Great Falls station because Richard hated the country music the local station played. She remembers the painfully afforded high school clothes she wore even though she knew the disarray that lay ahead for the perfectly pressed skirts and sweaters and white picot collars, and she remembers the insistent chords and rhythms, the textures of voices that filled the dark like layers when Ritchie Valens sang about love and pain and the endless dimensions that the next moment would bloom into. The next moment was what they were all headed for, all the cruising couples in the cars. If they couldn't touch it yet, they were reaching for it, and Jen remembers catching her breath as other headlights sliced the windshield and diffused in Richard's hair.

"Those awful people. What were their names? What they did to you. You don't know how often I've wondered whatever happened to you after that."

Their fresh drinks arrive, whiskey for Laura, a vodka tonic for Jen. Jen stirs, bites the maraschino cherry off its little parasol, and chews it. She thinks that Laura's already had one whiskey too many, or else she's been living too long in, where did she say she was living now, San Francisco or Seattle, where it's fashionable for people to spill their guts on short acquaintance.

"The way the story went around school, his folks drove you and Richard a hundred miles out of town, had the marriage performed in some little county courthouse, then drove home with Richard and left you there by yourself?"

"That's not quite how it happened," says Jen.

"I didn't suppose so."

Although that had been the plan. *We'll make sure that at least it has a name,* Richard's father had said, *which is the least we can do.*

And Jen remembers what she came here to remember. That if Richard's father hadn't forced her to sit in the back seat that morning, she might never have noticed how frail and pimpled the back of Richard's neck had looked between his white shirt collar and his fresh haircut.

At the time she had told herself she should have spoken up, she should have insisted on sitting beside Richard, but his father had been gunning the Chrysler's motor for several minutes in the alley behind her parents' house, and he had barely given her time to pull her feet in beside Richard's mother and close the door before he shot off. And there they were, the four of them in the Chrysler. In the front seat, Richard and his father, crammed to the explosion point into his tight suit and summer hat, and in the back seat, Richard's mother in flowered rayon, and Jen herself in her new nubby turquoise suit and nylon stockings and white pumps. There had been no next moments about to bloom. Nothing had pointed ahead but the highway.

"You," Jen says. "What's happened with you?"

"I'm an attorney. My firm's Seattle-based, but I get over to this side of the mountains several times a year. We do a lot of environmental work. You?"

"I'm an office manager for a firm in Billings. Petroleum firm."

Pondering their opposite sides of the great political and economic divide of the nineties, they drink their drinks in an uneasy silence that Laura finally breaks.

"Are you married?"

"Divorced twice. Just the one kid. You?"

"Divorced twice. One kid."

"You ladies want another drink?" asks the young bartender, swiping automatically with his towel. He's got a lovely smile—white teeth, dark face—and a tip jar crammed with dollar bills on the bar beside him.

"Why not?" says Laura. "This reunion's going nowhere." She props herself on the bar with one arm and swivels her stool so her back is turned to the sunlit door and her face obscured. Her eyes glitter, and Jen suddenly remembers the eyes of the coiled snake, unmoving and shiny as pinheads in the flat head.

"What really happened out there?"

What really happened.

Jen remembers that she'd had a choice between looking at the back of Richard's inadequate neck or looking out the window as the weeds in the borrow pit flowed into her past life, and so she watched the weeds liquefying to water until the illusion made her carsick, and then she stared into the distance. Sagebrush hills, a few fence lines. No signs of life, only a glimpse of an antelope with its ears pointed and its white rump catching the sun.

What did your father say? Richard's mother asks in a voice low enough not to be heard in the front seat.

That I can't live at home any longer.

It was the wrong answer, she knows from Richard's mother's face, but uppermost in Jen's mind at that moment is where she's going to sleep tonight. She isn't an antelope, after all, she can't just run off into the sagebrush.

"Where did they take you?" insists Laura, voice of the present.

Where.

They had driven a hundred miles when Richard's father turned off the highway on a gravel access road that billowed dust as it dropped down from the prairie into irrigated farmland, alfalfa in purple bloom and yellow sweet clover growing in the excess water that trickled through the borrow pits. A town of sorts lay ahead, a few buildings, scattered and random and small in the shadow of the rimrocks to the south.

Entering Windham, pop. 341.

Richard's mother leans forward, breathing heavily in the dust and heat. *My land, where'd they find three hundred and forty-one people left to count in Windham?*

Only thing that matters to me is that they still got their county courthouse, says Richard's father.

In front of a Quonset hut shaded by a grove of cotton-wood trees was a Portasign. Windham Food Mart, Special on Watermelon, and across the gravel street a Conoco station with two pumps. Then a few boarded-up buildings, a fence crammed with tumbleweeds, and an uninterrupted sweep of empty grass and gray sagebrush all the way to the gray rimrocks.

People live out here, whispers Jeanette.

Richard's father mimics her voice. *Yes, a few of them still live out here.*

They thought they was really going to have a town at one time, says Richard's mother. She shades her eyes with her hand, seeing what only she can see. *At the time of the Cat Creek oil strikes they had two, three thousand people living here. There's where our newspaper office was, and my father always said—*

Richard's father in his singsong, mimicking voice: *Yes, your father was a big newspaperman and Richard's going to major in journalism.*

Richard's mother says nothing more, and Jeanette realizes that what Richard's mother is for in his family is to make fun of.

"Keep talking. I know you're remembering."

At the far end of the single street, in the center of its own block, with its sidewalks swept and its native grass scythed to a neat, dry stubble, stood a square two-storied building of dressed stone. Richard's father had driven up and parked by the curb. When he killed the Chrysler's motor, Jeanette had heard silence. In such absence of sound and clarity of light she felt unreal inside her clothes, as though her face and hair and extremities had been reduced to blood cells and bone cells.

Going to be hot as an oven.

We ain't going to be here that long.

And all these sidewalks, says Richard's mother. Wincing at garters, she heaves herself out of the back seat. *Everybody's property taxes went to pay for these sidewalks, miles of sidewalks. But my father always said a town like Windham was going to need sidewalks.*

Your father always said! Your father always said!

Jeanette thought of running. Instead she walked with Richard and his father and mother up the stone steps. When she accidentally brushed Richard's hand, he gave her a wild-eyed look.

At the top of the steps Richard's father held open one of the modern plate-glass doors, and Jeanette saw a lobby of dark oak wainscoting with oak stairs rising into shadows. On the wall by the double glass doors hung a felt-board directory of county offices. Treasurer's office, superintendent of schools, justice of the peace. That was the point. There was still a justice of the peace out here, but no newspaper to publish the county vital statistics, no public record where anybody could count backward from the birth of the baby and find the date of the marriage license.

And what Jeanette will be for in this family will be to blame.

Richard's father pushed back his coat sleeve to consult his watch, and Jeanette saw the exposed white wrist and the separate black hairs rising like ants from the friction of the sleeve.

No, Jeanette says.

They turned and looked at her as blank as though they were seeing her lips move without hearing her voice. But Richard had taken her meaning. His mouth opened, starved and wordless, but Jeanette looked past him, through the glass doors where the sun shone on the courthouse steps and the shark fins of the parked Chrysler reflected the sidewalk. Across the street, the door to the tin-roofed building with the Budweiser sign had just opened and closed. Someone had just disappeared into the bar.

I'm going to be sick, she says. *Carsick. I'm going to throw up.*

"I've thought to this day," she tells Laura, "that if I'd begged them, if I'd cried and said I had nowhere else to go—"

"Which was the truth. Everybody in high school knew your father had kicked you out."

"—because they needed me. To blame. They'd have taken me home with them if I'd cried. They would have loved it if I'd cried."

Richard looked so sick that as recently as that morning she would have felt sorry for him, but now she walked—no, ran—past him, although the soft linoleum stuck like suction to the soles of her new white shoes. As memory and the reliving of memory blur, Jeanette's up against the glass door, she's pushing open the door, she can't believe that at the last moment a heavy hand with black hairs on its wrist won't descend on hers, but no, she's through the door now with her hand to her mouth as though she's running for the weeds to heave.

If she can just run as far as the thin line of noon shade behind the bar.

And she does. And in that sparse shade, out of sight, she pauses, gasping. The steel siding of the bar still retains some of its morning cool. A breath of air lifts her damp hair. She hears a grasshopper gnawing at dry stalks, gets a whiff of stale beer from a metal garbage can.

An outhouse leans out of the weeds, unused apparently, for its boards are as dry as bones. Jeanette thinks of her own room and her own bed with its clean sheets and pink blanket. Her fingertips remember the sticky varnish on the door of the bathroom at the end of the hall, a door that can be closed and locked for privacy, where light filters through a plastic shade and painted swans sail among water lilies over the pale green fixtures, tub and basin and toilet. She supposes that such comfortable illusions are a thing of the past for her.

A tiny path leads around the outhouse and through a gap in the fence. After a moment Jeanette tears herself from her precarious shelter behind the bar and follows the path. Puffs of dust rise under her white shoes. When she comes to the fence, she has to be careful not to snag her nylons on the tumbleweeds and broken wire. Her eyes have adjusted to the glare of sun on alkali. The rimrocks, she thinks. She can walk as far as the rimrocks.

And she does walk until, shoulder-deep in sagebrush, she looks back and sees how the random buildings—courthouse and bar and scattered houses with dry lawns—have been diminished by distance. The miniature smudged green of irrigated alfalfa fields and the gray thread of highway remind her of the way she came. From somewhere comes the whistle of a meadowlark, its six full notes lingering in the heat. Ahead are the rimrocks, but farther than she had thought. And when she looks down at her feet, she sees concrete, laid in straight lines except where it's crumbled at the edges over time. All those miles of sidewalks, she remembers, paid for with taxes. But she follows this sidewalk for a few yards, protecting her face with her arms where sagebrush has overgrown the concrete, until she comes to an intersection stamped with street names in the shade of bunchgrass. Imaginary streets, she realizes. She's walked into a new dimension.

A few boulders have drifted down from the rimrocks into the sagebrush to settle and sleep. Jeanette sits on the first boulder she comes to, finds it warm and gritty with sand.

Silence.

Coyotes, she supposes, could be out here. She's never seen one, although of course she's read about them. She savors the dangerous edges of the present, the sharpened blade of the near future. How long will Richard's parents wait? Will they follow her into the sage, or will they drive away without her? And Richard, what will become of Richard with no Jeanette to blame? But she can't concentrate on Richard. The sun beats down on her boulder. She yawns.

The sound that answers her yawn is registered instantly, although she has never heard anything like it. It's not a whirr or buzz of insects in harmless grass, not this rasp, which stills her.

Infinitesimally she turns her head, just a fraction to see behind her on the boulder, and even that tiny motion again elicits the angry rasp, the second warning.

Petrified, she yet takes in details, as though her senses, calmly relaying sights and sounds through the appropriate synapses, are continuing after the fact, like the heartbeat of the clinically dead. The dry rasp, the flat head, and the oiled patina over the power, like a single pulsing muscle, seemingly boneless, of the coiled rattlesnake.

The snake juts out its flat head, widening the wedge of its triangular jaw to display throat and fangs. Rattling, threatening, the head thrusts again, the tongue flicks. But what Jeanette cannot tear her eyes from—*run!* screams an electrical sensation down her backbone, *no! don't run! whatever you do, don't move!* screams another, instantaneous rebuttal—are the eyes of the snake, unmoving as pinheads and fixed on Jeanette.

The sun burns down, baking the grassheads, and somewhere the meadowlark whistles, but for Jeanette on the boulder, time has stopped. It occurs to her that the snake sees her, just as she sees the snake. If she could look closely enough, she could see herself reflected in the snake's eyes. And what does the snake see? A looming shape between itself and the sun? A blob of turquoise and white, an odor of fear and Avon Here's My Heart perfume? Can a snake see colors? Can a snake smell?

Jeanette sees the snake, yes, with its diamond patterns of red and orange and brown scales shading into cream on the underside of its coils. An underside that must feel the same gritty texture of the warm sandstone that Jeanette herself feels, and a pulse so vital that she would be drawn to touch it if the very thought didn't quicken her with waves of panic that wash down from her hairline and nearly blind her.

Run!

No! Don't run! Don't move!

Time passes. Time stands still. Jeanette no longer knows which of these statements is true. She seems to contain all time. From the faraway highway rises the round of a car accelerating, a rush of engine and air fading into distance, like a last echo of the world she has walked away from. Jeanette takes the slightest of breaths, shallow breaths that barely lift her white eyelet blouse off her chest. She thinks it might be the sun that affects her perceptions. The sun strikes the boulder with white heat. It radiates the bleached alkali flats and sends an illusion of water shimmering through the sage. In this excess of clarity, Jeanette squints and sees the miniature dark structures of the town begin to levitate and wobble. Jeanette really has walked farther than she had thought.

The snake rasps, poised to strike. Falling back to save herself, Jeanette finds herself flat on her back, staring up at the inexorable sun. Black shapes reel and spin through her vision. She turns her head and closes her eyes, remembering a long-ago teacher who had warned that looking directly into the sun might permanently damage her vision.

"My God! Had you been bitten?"

"No. I—no, as it turned out."

She listens to silence. The faint whisper of air currents through the sage leaves, the scratches of some minuscule animal in the bunchgrass, the whine of a gnat. With her eyes still closed, she slaps at the gnat. How far has she come? Then she remembers the snake, and her eyes snap open on a filigree of gray branches and gray leaves between herself and the sun.

"It was the damnedest thing. I found myself lying on concrete. I knew I'd walked in strange ways and back again."

"And drunk the milk of paradise," says Laura. "If I drink any more whiskey, I won't be able to stand up. But what about Richard? You and he never actually got married, then?"

"No. They waited for me for—oh, an hour or more, I think, before they gave up. Sorry. My tongue's too thick to talk. What I mean is, I never gave Richard any warning. No wonder he moped for years. Hell, no wonder guys are such sorry wrecks. I had just walked into another dimension, so to speak, and left him by his lonesome."

"I wish I'd had your guts. It took me a hell of a lot longer than that to walk away."

"Everybody but us has gone to sit at the banquet table. Do you think if we stand, we can hold each other up?"

"No. No. I want to know what else happened. How you—well, lived. Had the baby. And so on."

"Oh. Well, eventually I walked back into Windham. Sunburned. Sand in my clothes, stickers in my ass. There was a woman in the bar. I can still see the way she grinned when I told her what happened. Actually she's still there, she still runs the Windham bar. I always schlop, excuse me, stop to see her whenever I can. She—well. One thing and another. Come on, we're missing the class prophecy."

"You ladies had enough?" inquires the young bartender, snapping his towel.

Laura carefully slides off her barstool, wobbles. Fumbles in her purse, finds a dime, and drops it in his tip jar. She totters off for the banquet room and doesn't notice, but Jen sees him give her a look of purest hatred.

She stands up, brushes off her suit skirt, and twists it back into place. A strand of hair has caught in the bark of sage—no, no, this is the present, and she's drunker even than she thought. Hell yes, she can move her head. Back and shoulders feel okay. She searches for her shoes, finds one in a clump of bunchgrass, the other in a low-growing patch of eared cactus that has poked its way through the crumbling remains of those miles of sidewalks leading nowhere through the mirages. She shades her eyes. Yes, there is the horizon. She starts walking.

Varia's Revenge

Four young men in full camouflage gear walk along a country road with their rifles held at their hips and ready for anything. It's a scene from TV, or ought to be. The small screen would contain the autumnal smear of gold aspen leaves in the midst of dark green pines, the blue mountains in the middle distance, the clarity of the early morning sky. It would catch the dust puffing under the tramp of expensive boots, and then it would quick-cut to the tense faces of the young men as they swing their rifles in apprehension of this suspicious rustle in the ripened grass, that fugitive quiver through the pine needles. It's the tension in those young faces and yet their bland innocence, their lack of all lines or shades or complexities, that suggests the made-for-TV movie, but which? Can't be Vietnam again, there are no rice paddies, no bamboo. Maybe it's set somewhere in the Balkans, judging from the birch groves and the sunlit meadows that finger down between the timbered hills? Maybe it's one of those government-takeover thrillers in an all-purpose setting in middle America? Or maybe it's no drama, because this is northern Idaho, after all, and perhaps these grim young men with the inexperienced faces are paramilitary patriots on the move?

At a crackle in the underbrush, one of the young men spins and fires his rifle. Keerack-bang! The shot bursts the illusion of the TV movie. It's too head-splitting, too reverberating, too all-encompassing of space with sound to be anything less than real gunfire.

"What the hell were you shooting at, Larry?" says one of his companions, as the sound of the shot echoes between the pine hills and echoes again and finally fades.

"Dunno—I thought I saw something move."

I like to start my mornings with coffee and Ann Zwinger on the deck. At least it's been Zwinger I've been reading lately, and I have to say that she's one of my favorite nature writers because of the delicacy of her expression and the attention she pays to the smallest things, stonefly nymphs in cold-running mountain creeks, bloodworms hanging on in muddy backwaters, eggs and larvae and minute swarms of gnats. What for me is something to slap at is for Zwinger a part of the dance of the world, which is a good thing to be reminded of.

From my chair on the deck I can't see Bear Creek through the overhang of maple leaves unless I stir myself to get up and lean out over the railing, but I can hear the incessant splash of its current against the pilings under the footbridge, and I can smell the mint and the cress that grow wild along with the swamp grass and the blackberry brambles. Once the leaves have changed color and fallen, I'll have a better view, and after snowfall I can observe the tiny, private trails of mice and rabbits breaking through the crust and leading down to the water's edge. Even in the winter, with a cup of steaming coffee, a heavy blanket around my shoulders, and the white cloud of my own breath reminding me that I may have taken early retirement, but I'm still alive, and what more can I ask. An aged man is but a paltry thing, says Yeats, and what can an aged woman be but a paltrier one. But right now, now, in mid-October in northern Idaho, with a roof of bronzed and crisped leaves rustling over my head, with the sun coming up strong and promising real warmth by noon, with my horses grazing in the pasture below my house, within sight and sound and smell, I can almost truthfully tell myself that, after all these years, this is enough.

I lean over to slap at something invisible that's biting my ankle, one of Zwinger's tiny performers no doubt, and at that instant hear the whine, followed by the reverberation and the crystal sound of breaking glass, somehow in that order and yet simultaneously in the space between my poised hand and the slap, that pitches me off my chair into something between an obeisance and a crouch. For an interminable instant I'm face-down on the planks, staring through a knothole at weeds and gravel underneath the deck, then I'm raising my head in a supreme effort to see my coffee mug still perched whole and imperturbable on the deck rail, my book with its pages tumbled, and my shattered window.

"Hunting season," Jacob reminds me.

Local color, that's Jacob. During the year and a half that I've lived on Bear Creek, I've gotten into the habit, occasionally in the late afternoons, of walking across the footbridge behind my house and taking the trail across the horse pasture. At the bottom of the pasture, a stile straddles the three-strand barbed wire fence that divides my property from the old LeTellier place, where third-growth pines stretch and jab for space and sunlight on the slope. The first time I climbed the stile was this time last year, looking for pinecones. I was crouching on my knees in the layers of rusty needles, pushing my hair out of my face and breathing the late summer scent of warm turpentine, when I happened to glance up and notice the man on the porch of his frame house, watching me from a hundred yards away.

Oh god I'm trespassing, was all I could think. I'm stealing his pinecones.

But after a moment, seeing that I had seen him watching, he raised his hand in what might have been a benediction or a wave, and went back inside his house. And I felt chastened, but also relieved. I finished gathering enough pinecones to zing my wood fire with sparks and colors, green and gold, and I found a few large enough to sit in a row on my mantel, and then I took my sack and went home.

The next afternoon, driving home from the post office, I turned into the narrow road, not much more than a track, that led down through the sumac to his house, which I later learned was built by his grandfather, nearly a hundred years ago. It was set well back under the sycamores, ancient porch and narrow sash windows looking down on a strew of twigs, a world away from my raw new redwood and glass construction. I parked my new pickup under the biggest sycamore and knocked on the screen door.

"I'm Varia Noble," I said, when he came to the door. "I'm your neighbor on the hill, the one who took your pinecones."

The screen shadowed his face darkly, and I couldn't be sure of his expression. Fierce as I am about my own privacy, I was afraid I had violated his. Then too, there's a silent code of etiquette in these tiny north Idaho communities, where the same families have lived for three or four generations, and newcomers have no way of measuring their offenses.

But then he opened the screen door into the light, and I saw that he was an old cowboy in worn-out Levi's and boots that had had their original color scuffed off. He smiled, showing broken teeth, and offered his hand, formally.

"Jacob LeTellier," he said, which I already knew from the realtor who had sold me my land. And he invited me inside, limping ahead of me through a hall with a sloping floor and into a spare, square room with uncurtained windows, a cold woodstove, and an untidy stack of newspapers and journals on the floor by an oak rocking chair. That first afternoon he brought a straight chair out of the kitchen and offered me the rocking chair, and now the straight chair seems to live in the square room with the stove.

"It's the opening day of deer season," Jacob reminds me now, and I realize that yes, at this time last fall the stillness on Bear Creek had been shattered by the roar of expensive back-road vehicles and pickup trucks raising the dust on our lanes, with men in bright orange vests and orange caps carrying rifles and prowling the fringes of meadows or shade of timber at dawn or twilight, and, always, the distant, anonymous peppering of gunfire. My mares had shied and run at first and then gone back to grazing with unconcern.

But I've lost my unconcern. "That bullet broke my window! It just missed me! If I hadn't moved at that moment, it might not have missed me."

Jacob's seeing something beyond the walls of the room. I watch his eyes watching whatever it is. He watches it out of sight, then returns from wherever he's been.

"When I was a kid," he says, "we all knew not to shoot over a horizon, but these guys don't seem to know the same things we did."

"So they're dangerous! So what do I do? Can I just assume that no more than one bullet per hunting season is likely to buzz my deck?"

"Everybody on Bear Creek posts their land," he says, and yes, I've seen the No Hunting signs that have suddenly proliferated on my neighbors' fences and gates, not that they themselves don't hunt, but they do want to keep out the city riffraff. And for the first time I'm appreciating what they mean by riffraff. But what good is a No Hunting sign when a brainless somebody on a county road can fire a bullet from a rifle and not even know he's shattered a window a quarter of a mile away?

"But I've seen them," I insist. "Early this morning, four of them, walking along the road in camouflage, of all clothes to wear hunting, and carrying their rifles at their hips as if they thought they were combat soldiers. Anything they know, they've learned from TV. I'm going to call the county sheriff."

"Yes, you could do that."

He leaves unspoken the obvious. Without catching them in the act, what can the sheriff do about them? Instead he drinks the bitter dregs of his coffee, sets the mug down on the floor beside his rocker, and looks at his empty hands. Jacob is—oh god, younger than I am, I'm sure—in his fifties, maybe even his late forties. Dark-haired, dark-skinned, hawk-nosed. If he'd get his teeth capped he'd look younger, handsome even. He only shows his years in the constant pain lines in his face. Half his stomach shot away, I heard one of the neighbors say in the post office, and I'm not the only woman who thinks he's a doll—*yeah, he's got the eyes and the Levi's*, I heard one of them say. First time I'd ever heard that expression.

More post office gossip is that he hasn't always lived here, he came back from somewhere in Montana when the old man died. He puts in a big garden every year, keeps a saddle horse and runs a few cattle, but although I've never asked, I've always supposed that he must depend on some kind of disability money. Service in Vietnam, probably, from his age and the nature of his wounds and his silences.

But he sheers away from my sore points.

"Varia," he says, "you want to be sure to get that old pinto mare's teeth floated before snowfall. She's maybe not grazing any too good. I've been noticing that her ribs show."

"Oh, I'll be sure to do that! I've already called the vet!"

And I stand up so fast that my chair tilts wild and empty behind me. I gather up my coffee cup and Jacob's and carry them out to his lean-to kitchen where buckets of late tomatoes and cucumbers from his garden smell like the end of summer. I wish I knew how to nettle him into sharing my anger.

Getting old. As the popular wisdom has it, you're still the same person. Beneath the mane of white hair and the papery skin you're still the woman who once traded on her looks. But there's the shrinking of possibility, always. All the things you know you'll never do. Learn ancient Greek, practice the piano, tone your body into really good shape and make the Olympic riflery team. Get rich. Be famous.

Attract lovers.

The hardest part is living under the surface that other people see. Jacob is perhaps ten chronological years younger than I, which, because men retain their value for more years than women do, stretches to something like twenty years in practical time. If he's, say, forty-nine, he'd be looking for a woman in her thirties, and I'm sixty—actually, a thirty-year difference in practical time, and so what can I do but acquiesce to the weight of my years, acknowledge the erosion of my face and body, and bow out of the dance with what grace remains to me?

Jacob as I saw him a month or two after I first met him, before I knew him well. The pines on the ridge above the Bear Creek road were inky against the powder snow that had fallen in the night, and the sky was colorless and cold. I had been looking out my living room window, wondering what I'd been thinking of, moving to north Idaho where I would have locals for neighbors, and having this house built where I could lick my wounds and brood. A stir in the pines had caught my eye, snow falling from a bough as crows rose briefly, flapped and squawked and settled again.

Then the movement along the ridge, the three or four white-faced cows with grown calves trotting out of the timber ahead of the man on the horse. His coat collar was turned up and his hat pulled down, but I recognized the lanky brown gelding he was riding, I'd often seen that horse in the pasture below Jacob's barn when I drove to town and thought, no particular breeding there, maybe a strain of thoroughbred showing up in the length of those legs. And I saw that Jacob rode with a cowboy's flat seat in the saddle, reins held high and boots well forward in the stirrups. I watched as he glanced down the hill toward my house, although of course he couldn't see me standing in my window in my red robe, and then he rode into the pines and I was looking at an empty clearing.

And I remember thinking that, thirty years ago, even twenty years ago, I'd have taken that cowboy to bed with me for the slant of his hat and his seat in the saddle. I remember telling myself that it wouldn't have come to anything, of course. How could it, me with my M.B.A. and my executive track record and him just a piece of local color with, I suppose, at most a high school diploma.

It's not that I have designs on Jacob, no, of course not, but I allow myself, on carefully spaced occasions, to sit in the same room with Jacob, to take pleasure in his face and the iron composure of his hands, his secret wounds and the long spaces between his words. Always in Jacob there is the dark male other, the banked fire that has always drawn me. If I lust for Jacob, if I burn, let it be my secret, let me keep what dignity I can.

The old pinto mare, as Jacob calls her. She raises her head and nickers to me as, waist-deep in wild grass, I cut across the pasture to the footbridge. She turned twenty-five this spring, a horse's old age, and although her finely drawn dark eyes and sweep of black forelock look unchanged to me, her sagging belly reminds me of her years and the many foals she has borne. When I put my arms around her neck, she buries her face in my shoulder, and I smell the deep horse odors of sweat and grass-manure.

"Sophie, you're as old as I am."

The white patch on her shoulder spreads into her mane, as white and coarse as my own hair has turned, although my hair already was streaked with white on the day I delivered her. I was thirty-five and long-limbed and supple then, and she was a wet and wobbly pinto foal into whose nose and mouth and ears I thrust my fingers to imprint her with my touch and scent, while her mother, poor long-dead Sallie, hovered over us and soughed and whickered with all the tender gutturals that a mare utters to a newborn. Sophie, I named the foal, wanting an S name to connect her with her mother.

Those damned horses of yours, Glenn called them. Damned-horses, as though *damned* was stuck to *horses* without the possibility of hope or redemption. But Glenn is long gone, to Canada during the Vietnam draft, and never came back, and we're still together, my old companion Sophie and me, she swishing her tail and I musing on mortality in the luck of a sunlit October meadow, where the aspens rustle and whisper of hard frosts to come, and Sophie's daughter Tara (I couldn't think of another S name I liked) raising her head from grazing at the bottom of the slope and listening for meaning carried on currents of air that I'll never hear.

And I tell myself once again, this is enough. Warm horsehair, the small sounds of late insects in tall grass, Sophie's head in my arms, the pulse in her neck. Her vulnerability, her trust. This is enough.

* * *

Strapping tape and a flap from the red cardboard carton that the coffee came in covers the hole in the window for now. I've called Steve at Quality Glass in town, and he has promised to send somebody out in the morning to install new glass, and I suppose it's going to cost a small fortune, because it's less a window than a glass wall that I had designed into the living room for the view. Steve's reaction made me feel a little better—"Bullet through your window? Them goddamn out-of-state hunters! They don't know a goddamn thing about firearms, they're going to kill somebody yet"—but when I discover that I cannot sit in my leather armchair with my back to the glass wall without flinching, I'm furious again and dial the county sheriff's number and actually get the sheriff himself on the line.

The sheriff, who's too young to call a good old boy, was narrowly elected to office last November after a fierce race against a former police chief from Coeur d'Alene. He commiserates with me. "It's a damn shame, pardon me Miss Noble, when a lady like you can't drink her coffee on her own deck without some fool firing off a bullet in her direction. People from around here, now, they understand about firearms. It's these assholes from out of state, pardon me for putting it like that, but it happens every fall. They come over to Idaho from Seattle or Spokane, and all they think about is, blast away at whatever moves."

Sure, he'll keep an eye out. Maybe I hadn't noticed, but he's had extra deputies on the county roads since dawn, and the boys from Fish and Game have also been out in force. Reckless use of firearms is what they're watching for, that, and hunting without a valid Idaho license, because another thing these Seattle and Spokane hunters like to do is try to get away without paying their out-of-state hunting fees. But he wants me to know that out here we've got a whole lot of back roads to cover, and the hell of it is that if you don't catch the individuals in the act, it's hard to prove they did it—unless, of course, there's a bullet to match with a gun. I hadn't happened to find the bullet, had I?

No.

But I do find it, later that evening when, sitting in my armchair pulled around by the brass reading lamp, glass of whiskey at hand and my book in my lap, well away from the night-blackened window with its incongruent red patch, I notice a miniature pyramid of white dust on the oak floorboards, realize that it must have trickled down from the wall above the trophy case, go to investigate, and then go to the kitchen to get a paring knife and pry the lump out of the wall.

Curious, I hold the misshapen little lump in the palm of my hand, wondering if I would recognize it as a bullet if I didn't already know. Mud-colored, disproportionately heavy, a seed of destruction. I weigh its spent power, examine it from all sides, finally touch my tongue to it and feel saliva rush through my mouth at the acerbic thrill in the taste of metal. How odd it is that, after all my years of loading and firing rifles, this is the first spent bullet that I have ever seen or touched.

Safety, safety, safety was what our instructors drilled into all their riflery students. Never assume a rifle is unloaded unless you personally have broken it and checked. Never set down a rifle without checking it. Never point a rifle at anything you don't intend to fire at. Never, never walk onto a firing range without calling for broken rifles. And I, in their classes and later in competition, observed their rules as meticulously as I measured my firing patterns on my targets and fired and fired again.

Fired joyously, just as Glenn accused me.

Competition shooting, he said bitterly. You can call it a competitive sport, he said, but you know good and well what its purpose is. How you can bear to engage yourself with an instrument whose sole purpose is to cause harm is more than I know.

Now, as I cast around this room that I've furnished with the relics of my life, the scarred leather chairs and the Kharastan carpet that I lugged all the way back from Turkey in 1969, the war masks from Cameroon, and the spears, and the paintings from everywhere, in the warmth of brass lamps and books and the textures of river rock and polished oak, I try to imagine what I might say to Glenn about a young sheriff's condescension to a woman with white hair. About these new, ignorant riflemen of the late twentieth century. About all my years as an executive when my spontaneity was a liability and rage a bad luxury, and about those last humiliating months in Boise before I finally bowed to the inevitable and opted for early retirement from Microdesign.

About the glow of my present anger. About the red patch on the window that seems to shift and throb, until I see it darkly as the ruby-red of blood.

This time it's not the whine of the bullet that I hear in the endless instant, but the crash of the rifle, and from my chair on the deck I watch Sophie fling up her head, leap as though she's been struck by a sudden aspiration, and collapse into the grass. Crash of coffee mug, flutter of pages. At the bottom of the deck stairs I trip on terrace stones, land on all fours, knees of my blue jeans torn and the skin torn off the palms of my hands, but I'm up and running, and the heavy grass drags at my legs, it's like one of those dreams where you can't run, and I'm not even thinking about whether he'll take a shot at me or not, but by the time I reach Sophie, even the fugitive movement in her legs has stopped.

I hold her head in my arms, but I can't tell whether she recognizes me or not. The light in her lovely, velvet eyes is fading, then gone. Oh Sophie Sophie and my eyes are a blur of tears, but when a shadow falls between me and the clean early morning sunlight I look up from my beautiful dead Sophie and see the boy in his camouflage clothing, holding his rifle and bending over us.

"I knew I hit something," he says.

"You son of a bitch!" I scream.

"Hey now!" he says, startled. "Where's my deer?"

I swear to God that's what he says. He's all the clichés come true, the story somebody told in the post office about the preacher's horse getting shot out from under him and the hunter running up and yelling, *get your saddle off my elk,* a story I hadn't believed, but then I wouldn't have believed experiencing this long moment of clicks, as separate and slow as frames of film, as I give myself to pure, pure rage. It's not because screaming at him might bring her back, oh Sophie Sophie Sophie, but because it's a rush, a shrieking runaway locomotive drive out of all reason, moderation, and self-control. It's elation, it's intoxication, it's a transportation into that red realm I always knew about but never entered until now.

And yet, through the glaze I can see his startled young face; he's wondering what the old woman with the streaming eyes and the wild white hair is yelling about; he sees the blood on her face and knees and hands and he takes an involuntary step backward because he fears the power of the crone and not because it's sunk into him that he's done anything wrong. And stepping backward, he stumbles against something, a rock hidden in the wild grass maybe, I don't know, although all sequence for me is still in slow motion. In slow motion I see his hunting rifle tip in a slow arc in one direction as he falls in the other direction and a part of me waits for the shot that ought to be jarred out of the falling rifle, but no, I watch as it slowly slowly settles in a cushion of grass and wild asters, and then, as though I've rehearsed it, the uncoiling to my feet and the single swift strike that it takes, I'm in firing stance with the rifle at the ready and aimed at the young man's heart.

"God, lady," he says from flat on his back, "I didn't mean to do anything wrong."

"You asshole. You bastard. Get on your feet."

"Lady?" he says, getting up. "Just give me the gun?"

He gets up and takes that first step toward me, his hand outstretched, and it's a well-kept hand with clean fingernails, I have time to notice, as, trusting to the rifle's action and those old sequences drilled into me as deep as instinct, I draw my bead on the blond hair, damp and matted from the camouflage cap that fell off when he fell—*oh, reason! reason! reason! never point a gun at anything you don't intend to shoot*—raise the sights just a hair, and squeeze off my shot.

"Jesuschrist—" he hits the grass again, flat.

"On your feet, asshole. Hands over your head."

He does it. He actually scrabbles to his feet, panicky, and locks his hands over his head like a prisoner in a combat film, which I realize is where my lines must be coming from.

"Any funny moves, and I'll drill a hole through you. Start walking downhill, now, nice and slow."

And he does. He leads the way through the deep grass in a peculiar high-stepping gait with his buttocks tight and tucked in as if to ward off the bullet.

I think about drilling a bullet through his buttocks, how much joy it would be. But I can't quite do it. As long as I can keep the rifle trained on him, as long as we can keep walking, I'm not quite dying inside for beautiful, beautiful Sophie. Oh Sophie. The thought of her infuses me with a terrible sense of justification.

"Lady," he says, "I'm only twenty-two."

"You bastard, she was twenty-five."

He walks a little faster. Something tells me he's going to make a run for it, and I clear my throat harshly, just to remind him that the crone with the rifle is still following him, but the sound seems only to panic him, because he breaks into a high-kneed gallop with his hands, oddly enough, still clasped over his head, and I break every rule of riflery and fire at his feet.

The grass to the left of him thrashes from the impact of the bullet, and so does he, every bit as involuntary as poor Sophie but not as dead. I may just have clipped him in the ankle with my shot, or maybe not. Wah-wah-wah he's crying, like a little kid, and squirming around to see if blood is running out of his boot.

If I stopped to think about what I'm doing, I'd be done for, but I don't stop. "Crawl if you have to, bastard. That's right, over the stile."

He crawls, sobbing. I can't see any blood, but he has soiled the seat of his pants.

I drive him along the fence past Jacob's house and down the old trail through brambles and star thistles that rake the whimpers out of him. A few yards downhill, in the shade of sycamores and studded with bedraggled hollyhocks grown from generations of volunteer seed, leans the ancient outhouse that hasn't been used, I suppose, since Jacob's grandfather first had the house plumbed.

Old man LeTellier built a solid outhouse, however, of oak planks that have weathered to silver over the years but remain perfectly sound. The door hangs ajar, but although the space inside is dense with spiderwebs in all its corners, it's reasonably roomy, a three-holer. Any stink of outhouse has long dried up. It smells of the fall of the year, dusty and sweet.

"Lady, please!"

"In there, asshole."

I prod him with the rifle to keep him crawling, through the rustling hollyhocks and far enough inside the outhouse that I can shut the door on him. I prop it shut with the rifle, look around for a better wedge, and find a cedar fence post lying in the grass. Typical Bear Creek, all materials at hand. I drag the post over to the outhouse, wedge it against the door, and pound it firm with a rock.

In this boy's shape, it'll be a long time before he forces his way out. I can hear him crying as I walk up the trail through the weeds.

At the bridge I throw his rifle into the water and watch the current topple it for a few rushing yards over the clear gravel bottom. At the far end of the pasture, Tara has backed herself into the fence, snorting and lifting her feet as though she's about to go airborne. She smells Sophie's death, I know, but I don't have space in my thoughts for Tara yet. I wade through the sun-tipped grass to the silent mound, my Sophie. Her big body is still warm. After a moment I lie down beside her. My Sophie.

In the late afternoon, with the last of the fall sunlight glowing on the meadow grass like a false promise, a new four-wheel-drive outfit pulls into my driveway and three young men in laced boots and full camouflage, caps and all, climb out and scan pine ridges, pasture, road and the soft blue shoulders of mountains as though they expect to witness a materialization in thin October air.

One of the young men sees me watching from my deck and says something to his companions. They all turn to look, and for a moment their young faces and slack mouths mirror me, the crone in blue jeans with the glass of whiskey in her hand. Her swollen red eyes and her uncombed white hair caught with twigs and grassheads, bits of star thistle, perhaps even a scarlet hollyhock blossom, lit to fire by the late sun.

"Ma'am?" one of them finally asks. "You haven't seen a man on foot?"

"Sure haven't."

And it's technically true, he was on all fours the last I saw of him.

The young men shift uneasily, finally climb back into their big outfit. I see them glance over their shoulders at me as they pull out of my drive.

I go back to my whiskey—I can't concentrate on Zwinger, I keep seeing Sophie between the lines—but as evening turns to dusk and chill air rises from the creek, I hear a nighthawk calling, and occasionally the cries of the young men.

"Larry!"

"Larry!"

"Larry!"

Early next morning, before I've dressed and had my coffee, a black Bronco comes roaring up the Bear Creek road, brakes in a commotion of dust and gravel, and takes the sharp turn into my driveway. Its doors blaze with the county seal in stenciled gold, its roof bristles with red bubble lights. When I lean over the rail of my deck in my robe, shoving back my hair with both hands to see what's happening, the automatic window on the driver's side of the Bronco slides down and the sheriff sticks his head out.

"Miss Noble, we got a report on a missing hunter out here. Nobody's seen him since yesterday morning."

"Really."

"Haven't seen or heard anything, have you?"

Only the pounding of my heart, the dark edges of my vision.

"A party of guys came down from Spokane for opening day. Thought they might have better luck if they fanned out. They agreed to meet in the bar in Elk Park at the end of the day. One of them never showed up."

A large part of me, I'm just beginning to realize, must have died sometime during the past night of horrors. Went wherever Sophie went, or flew away with the owls, or dissolved in whiskey

fumes, all my sober years. But the ghost of my cool judgment reminds me that the sheriff is also a young and inexperienced male.
It shows in the way he bites off his words with a toughness he
wouldn't have to try for if he really had it.

His eyes search my house and deck, wander off toward the
pasture. "You don't mind if I walk down through your yard to the
crick, do you? Have myself a look-see?"

"Go right ahead."

I watch as he walks around my new double horse trailer,
which wrenches at my heart with its reminder of my *two* horses,
and hikes down the hill into the high grass, where the early morning sunlight glitters on the dissolving frost and gilds his shaggy
blond hair and the back of his gray uniform shirt. My coffee has
gone cold, but I don't want to go back in the house and reheat it.
Animal cunning replaced my reason last night, as the whiskey finally wore off, and brought me news of what I'd actually done,
and now I realize that the sheriff's visit means that I've still got a
prisoner in Jacob's outhouse.

The sheriff returns with his pant legs wet to the knees,
looking thoughtful. He leans on the post at the foot of the deck
stairs, regards me. His eyes are a pure blue, his face as unmarked
by years as the faces of the hunters, and I think about the impulses
of inexperience, about the young executives at Microdesign who
replaced me, and I shudder.

"What happened to your horse?"

It's too much, I burst into tears. "I'll try to hire somebody
with a backhoe and bury her."

"Don't worry about it, Miss Noble, don't cry, we'll get her
taken care of for you. It looked like a bullet hit her to me. You hear
any shots around here this morning?"

"Yesterday. I—"

"The assholes," the sheriff says. "Pardon my French, Miss Noble, but the damn fools, wearing camouflage, I couldn't believe my eyes when I saw them. The strange thing is that nobody shot one of them, thinking he was a deer. Or maybe somebody did, and that's why one of them hasn't turned up."

He stands there, leaning on the post, looking up at me, until I wonder if I've been too hasty in judging his inexperience.

"If that's what somebody did," he says, "it's a pity they didn't shoot him before he shot your horse. He must have thought he'd finally bagged his buck deer. But he must have panicked when he saw what he'd done, because he threw away his gun and ran right out from under his cap."

And the sheriff hands me the camouflage cap, damp from its night in the grass but otherwise stiff and new.

"His rifle's down there in the crick," he says. "I'm going back to town to get my waders, and then I'll drag it out of there."

Now I am in a quandary. As the sheriff's Bronco pulls out of my driveway with a flourish of gravel under its tires, I pace up and down the deck. At moments during the night I had been able, almost, to convince myself that I hadn't kidnapped a grown man at gunpoint and locked him in Jacob's outhouse. With the break of day it had seemed even more unlikely. Not something I'd ever do! Varia Noble with her M.B.A.! Who would believe it who had known her as a vice president for Microdesign, renowned for her level head and her cool decisions? No, not Varia Noble, who kept her dignity and her own counsel even under the pressure of those straining last months in Boise.

But then the awful truth would settle on me with the weight of a boulder, and worse thoughts would crowd in. What if I'd put a bullet through him? What if I'd killed him?

And now I begin to wonder if, in fact, that's what happened, that I really did nick him in the ankle, exploding an artery which filled his boot with blood (explaining why I hadn't noticed him bleeding), so that he then bled his life away among the spiderwebs in the dark. Because if he was still alive, he'd be raising a fuss, wouldn't he? Trying to escape? I know I wedged that post against the door good and solid, but after all, the outhouse is a hundred years old. It must have a rotten timber or two in its frame that wouldn't stand up to a good kicking with a booted foot.

But say he couldn't escape. If he yelled loud enough and long enough, Jacob would have heard him, wouldn't he? Jacob's hearing is a little dull, but not that dull, and the outhouse isn't that far from his back door.

I imagine Jacob reading in his rocker with his glasses on, thinking that he hears owls, getting up to toss another chunk of wood into his stove, and finally folding his glasses into his shirt pocket and going to the door to listen. By now it's fully dark and starlit, the sycamore leaves moving overhead, and he stands in the doorway for a moment, tasting the promise of snow in the chill air. Another Idaho winter on the way, be time to ship cattle before he knows it. No, whatever he's hearing, it's not an owl. The cries are human and frantic, beginning to sound hoarse, and so Jacob gets his flashlight out of his truck and goes to investigate. Led by the desperate cries, he finds himself following the old outhouse trail.

And then, seeing the post wedged against the door where no post belonged, hearing the kicks and yells and—well, Jacob would have let him out, wouldn't he? Jacob would have had no way of knowing that the captive boy had shot my mare, and even if he had known, what else would he have done?

I imagine the boy hammering on the door from the inside, as Jacob pries away the post and tosses it into the dark. The door falls open and the boy bursts out, white-faced in the flashlight beam, shaking from his escape attempts and smelling of fear.

What the hell's going on, Jacob might say.

A crazy woman, the boy would say. Took my gun away from me and forced me in here, blocked the door. Thought I'd never make anybody hear me.

A crazy woman.

I have to call my friends, the boy would say. They'll be worried sick by this time. If they haven't gone back to Spokane without me. Have you got a telephone? There must be some law enforcement somewhere, even in this godforsaken neck of the woods. It must be against some law, what she did to me.

Jacob would have led him back up the trail through the shadows of star thistles, trying to make sense of his story. Brought him into the house to warm himself by the woodstove, brought him the telephone on its long cord from the kitchen.

And the sheriff, so notified, would have driven out to Bear Creek at whatever hour. Knocked on my door. Grim-faced.

Would anybody in the world believe that the death of a horse was an extenuating circumstance?

But if he's *dead*.

I can't bear to walk past Sophie's body, which is beginning to bloat in the strengthening sun, so I walk around the edge of the pasture, by the fence. Even at that distance I can hear the blowflies. Tara raises her head from grazing and whinnies to me, trots to the fence and lays her head on my shoulder. Like Sophie she's just under fifteen hands; I've always preferred to ride a smallish horse. Her eyes so like Sophie's, dark and lashed, her head black like Sophie's, with a splash of white in the mane that splits into lightning stripes down her forelegs and over her flanks. When a fly lights on her shoulder, she shudders it off with a reflexive ripple of her hide.

I believe that horses feel affection and grief, and who is to say that Tara's is not the more intense for being the more bewildering. But a part of my consciousness is still too sore to touch, and my thoughts shy away, spin into a crazier cycle. What I've done. What will happen to me. When I leave Tara and follow the little overgrown trail behind Jacob's house, the spines of thistles scratch against my blue jeans and a low-hanging alder branch slaps at my face with a handful of wet dead leaves.

When I look back, I can see Jacob's upstairs window through the tops of the sycamores, blank panes of glass catching the morning sun and throwing it back. But no cries for help from the outhouse, no signs of distress. I'm the only disturbance on this trail.

The door of the outhouse hangs ajar.

Inside, a wreckage of spiderwebs and fresh gouges on silvery old planks. Of course he had a knife, I hadn't thought of a knife, but now I see the hacks in the oak boards where he tried to carve his way out. But the oak had resisted, he hadn't rescued himself.

No, he was rescued. The post has been taken from the door, tossed aside among the frost-draggled hollyhocks.

Had to be Jacob.

The walk of confrontation. The last time I walked that walk was down the paneled corridor to the president's office at Microdesign. That time, at least I could tell myself that I held the high moral ground. This time I have to march myself back up the trail through the star thistles and the overgrown grass. Jacob's garden, I pause to notice, is doing well in spite of our recent frosts. Tomatoes in varying degrees of ripeness hang from stakes with their leaves blackened, and pumpkins and squashes have proliferated over the carrot and onion rows, all enclosed from the rest of the world in a tidy rectangle of woven wire.

In the past he's been generous with his produce. Whenever I've visited, he's had a plastic sack ready for me with new peas, the first new potatoes, fresh tarragon even. Green onions. Tomatoes.

As I watch, a small brown bird, maybe a chickadee, lights with a bird's suddenness on a dirt clod where Jacob has been digging onions. It eyes me briefly, takes two or three hops, and pecks at something invisible among the stalks.

Well. I tramp along the garden fence and over the sycamore twigs that litter Jacob's yard. I've raised my fist to knock on his door, when it opens.

"Varia," says Jacob. He doesn't sound surprised. Well, he wouldn't be surprised, he's used to my dropping in at my carefully spaced intervals.

"The boy in the outhouse," I blurt.

Jacob just stands in his doorway for a moment, holding his first cup of coffee of the morning. The hot coffee is sending up a thin plume of steam in the tinge of frost, but Jacob's looking over my shoulder at something that's miles or years away from Bear Creek, and there's a sadness in his face, maybe a resignation, exhaustion even, that I realize has been there since I've known him. And yet I can't help noticing how very good-looking he is. The dark eyes, the dark hair hardly touched with gray. There's some Indian blood in the LeTelliers, is what they say in the Bear Creek post office, and when I first heard the story, it made Jacob seem all the more exotic to me, all the more attractive. In my present state of mind, I excoriate myself for romanticizing the man, for lusting after my image of him, while all the time I accepted the companionship of the real Jacob.

"The old pinto mare," he says after a while, still looking over my shoulder.

And I can't help it, I can feel the tears well up, and Jacob stoops to set his coffee cup on the doorstep, straightens again and puts an arm around my shoulder, awkwardly, and that does it, I'm crying like I never cried in my life, the way I never cried when Glenn left me or all the other men who left me because I was too damned competent or too damned independent or too damned self-centered or whatever their damned reasons were. Jacob smells of woodsmoke, of the garden earth on his hands, and of male sweat, which reminds me, and I pull away.

"My cousin-in-law's got a backhoe," he says. "We'll take care of her for you."

"The boy in the outhouse."

"What boy in the outhouse?"

"Jacob!"

"Oh, hell, Varia," he says. "Maybe I did talk to some kid last night," he says. "Late last night. Come to think about it, he did say something about a run-in he'd had with somebody."

"Jacob! It was a terrible thing I did."

"Varia," he says. "I've seen terrible."

And I suppose Vietnam, the one real trauma of our generation, and maybe he reads that on my face, because he says, "War isn't all that's terrible."

I'm remembering my rage, the joy of it, the cackling humor even, that interrupted my whiskey thoughts in the night with the image of the boy in camouflage crawling on his hands and knees through the thistles with the seat of his pants wet and darkly stained.

"Varia," says Jacob. "I think he knows what he did."

I pull away. "I know what I did."

I haven't switched on the lights or even touched a match to the kindling under the logs, but, huddled in the big leather armchair with my glass of whiskey and my thoughts, I watch the moon rise over the ridge and remember a story Jacob once told me, about the time the FAA took his pilot's license away from him.

It was a goddamn lapse of judgment, he said. Pilot error. I was the asshole that thought it couldn't happen to me, and that's why the FAA yanked my license. *Rescue* was what everybody in town thought it was. A poor little sick girl, and I risked my life for her. Hell, I was a hometown hero for a while.

Now the moon rides as high as a silver dime over the points of the pines, and I'm drinking whiskey in the dark and listening to the owls when there's a knock on my door. I give myself just a heartbeat to make sure I'm steady on my feet and go to answer.

It's Jacob, I recognize him by his silhouette. I flip on the entryway light and invite him in, and he carefully wipes his battered cowboy boots on the mat before he limps inside and looks around, shyly, at the room with the leather chairs and the stone-cold fireplace, the masks and the trophies and the bright colors of rugs and books.

"Always did wonder what it looked like inside this house," he says.

He walks over to the fireplace, touches one of the Cameroon spears, and I remember another story of his, about a woman he lived with over in Montana, a college professor, and how I'd thought, yes, she probably thought he was all eyes and Levi's, too.

"Varia," he says with his back turned, "here on Bear Creek the neighbors believe in sticking together."

"Meaning what? That nobody's going to charge me with kidnapping that boy at gunpoint because he's from *Spokane?*"

"He shot your horse."

"And the sheriff, what's he going to do, conspire to cover it up?"

"Holy Christ, it's cold enough in here to freeze my ass off," he says. "Any reason not to light this fire?"

"Go ahead, light it. I *shot* at him. What am I supposed to do, learn to live with it?"

With his knee on the hearth, he turns from striking a match and touching it to newspaper, which blazes up and illuminates the whites of his eyes and his teeth when he grins at me, and I feel like kicking him for it.

"Were you thinking you had some other choice but live with it?"

The dance of the world. I shake my head, I'm past speech.

"And another thing, do you think that kid wants to stand up in court and tell the world that he shot an old white-haired lady's horse, thinking it was a deer, and that the old lady took his own gun away from him and shut him up in an outhouse until she could call the sheriff to come and get him?"

"I *shot* at him."

"Yeah, I know, you already said that."

The son of a bitch, he's struggling to keep from laughing at me. And he's losing the struggle. He's laughing as, in the fireplace, the kindling dances in flames over the ashes of newspaper and spreads gold and red tongues over the logs, which crackle as a knot explodes into sparks. I think of my rage and how it burgeoned, and how close I was to murder and how joyful it felt. Maybe I might as well kill Jacob while I'm at it, kill him for laughing at me.

"I'm sorry," he says, "that I called you an old white-haired lady. Hell, you look pretty good to me, Varia. You look fine."

He says, "I'll go with you to the sheriff tomorrow if you think that's what you have to do."

"I do think that's what I have to do."

And I ask myself if there's any way I can accept the forgiveness that Jacob is offering. I'll saddle Tara in the morning, but I'll always grieve for Sophie. I'll always remember what I've done. A goddamn lack of judgment, was that what it was? Or just my part in the dance of the world? Or a warning, what I'm capable of.

He says, "You got any more of that whiskey you been swilling down?"

And I hear myself say it. "Oh hell, Jacob. You do have the eyes and the Levi's."